The Bower Bird

By the same author:

Because We Have Reached That Place, Oversteps Books, 2006 (poems)
The Burying Beetle, Luath Press, 2005 (a novel)
Sea Front, Truran, 2005 (photographs)
Paper Whites, London Magazine Editions, 2001 (poems and photographs)
The Poetry Remedy, Patten Press, 1999
Nine Lives, Halsgrove (audio book (stories)
Born and Bred, Cornwall Books, 1988 (photographs)

The Bower Bird

ANN KELLEY

Luath Press Limited

EDINBURGH

www.luath.co.uk

Thanks to Jutta Laing and the RD Laing Trust for permission to
reproduce material from *Conversations With Children*; and to Curtis
Brown, on behalf of the Estate of AA Milne, for permission to quote
from *Winnie Ille Pu*.

First published 2007

ISBN (10): 1-905222-79-3
ISBN (13): 978-1-9-05222-79-7

The author's right to be identified as author of this book
under the Copyright, Designs and Patents Act 1988 has been asserted.

The paper used in this book is neutral-sized and recyclable.
It is made from elemental chlorine free pulps
sourced from renewable forests.

The publisher acknowledges subsidy from
Scottish
Arts Council
towards the publication of this volume.

Printed and bound by Bell & Bain Ltd., Glasgow
Typeset in 11 point Sabon

For my wonderful family

PROLOGUE

I'm not dead yet.

CHAPTER ONE

WE'VE BEEN HERE for two weeks. I'm still not well enough to start at the local school. But the weather has been barmy – or is it balmy? Yes, it probably is balmy. Barmy means daft. The sun has shone on us most days since we moved, and I feel that my heart is going to mend enough to have the operation that could give me a few more years of life.

It's a cold night and the sky is clear. Stars are appearing one by one. I wear my distance specs to see them otherwise it's all a beautiful blur. I sit in my window on a stripy cushion and feel... happy.

The lights of the little town are twinkling below me, and there is a nearly full moon – its blue-white wedding veil draped across the bay. The lighthouse winks its bright eye every ten seconds.

I did have a bedside lamp on but moths kept coming in the window to commit suicide. Why do insects that choose to fly around in total darkness have a fatal attraction for hot light bulbs? They must be barmy. Or maybe a hot bulb gives off a smell like female moths and the male moths are attracted to it for that reason.

Even in the middle of the night seagulls are flying all around us, calling to each other in the dark. The wind has got up and the gulls are lifting on invisible currents and then swoop fast like shooting stars.

Our young gull is crouched on the ridge of the roof, his head poking out over the top, watching the adults and whining pathetically. There must be some juvenile gulls up there learning how to fly and land cleanly on the rooftops and chimneys, just as if they are alighting on cliff ledges.

I scrunch up under a warm woolly blanket with my feet

up, and Charlie keeps trying to get comfortable but there's no horizontal bit. She prefers me to be flat in bed so she can warm herself on my tummy, or my chest. She shouldn't really sit on my chest as I have trouble breathing at the best of times and anyway, I had open-heart surgery last year, when I was eleven, and the healing process hasn't finished yet. The operation was a waste of time. It was supposed to be one of three procedures to repair the various heart defects. When I was opened up they could see that I had no pulmonary artery, not even an excuse for one, and there was nothing to build on. So the surgeon just closed me up again. I now have an amazing scar that cuts me in half almost, as if I have survived a shark attack.

Poor Charlie, she doesn't understand why I don't want her on my chest.

I reluctantly leave the starlit night and get into my bed. I'm reading a really good book by Mary Webb called *Gone to Earth*. It's about a girl who has a pet fox. Mary Webb has written several other books. I'll have to look out for them at car boot sales or in the second-hand bookshop, as they are so old they are probably out of print.

As usual, the three cats wake me. Charlie is the noisiest and the most demanding. As soon as there's a glimmer of daylight she starts on at me to get up and feed her. She meows loudly and jumps on the bed and marches up and down on one spot, as if I am her mother and she is trying to make the milk come. She sound quite cross. If I pretend to sleep she gets really irate. The other two are more patient but they stare, accusingly. I can feel their eyes on me. Flo sits on the chest of drawers and Rambo on the window seat.

I wake to a completely pink dawn. Outside everything is saturated with an intense rosy glow. Pink sky, sea and bay. Pink roofs, candy sand. I yearned for a party dress when I was five or six, of exactly this shade – to match my Barbie doll's outfit.

By the time I find my specs, put on a dressing gown and flip-flops, load a film into my camera and lean out the window, the pink has paled and silvered, but the sun now hangs heavily above the dunes, like a red balloon full of liquid. One small boat chugs out of the harbour dragging a pink wake and gulls are following in a raucous rush.

I am surrounded by hungry cats. I better give in. Charlie is jubilant, running ahead down the stairs, calling me to hurry up. The others follow behind me.

I have to go to the bathroom first, and this really makes Charlie cross. She never knows whether to come in with me at this point, because she usually spends bath-time with me, but now she can only think about her rumbling stomach.

Mum is in the bathroom for longer and longer every morning. What does she do in there? She told me once that she hadn't had a decent crap since I was born. First I screamed all the time, then as I got bigger I banged on the door and yelled. When I was a baby I screamed for twenty-one hours once – she wasn't in the bathroom all that time, of course. She says I'm lucky to be alive as she nearly strangled me several times. Sleep deprivation makes you go barmy apparently.

'Mum, I have to wee, I'm desperate.'

She's looking into a magnifying mirror and doing something disgusting with scissors up her nose.

'Ohmygod, Mum, that's gross. You'll slice through your mucus membranes.'

'They're blunt-ended, Gussie. You wait until you get hairy nostrils. See how you like it.'

Hopefully I won't live that long.

She does all this other stuff, too, to her face, plucking and scraping and applying various very expensive unguents.

What a lovely word – unguents.

'Is it worth it, Mum?'

'Probably not, but I'm not giving up just yet.'

She's actually quite cool looking, I think, but because she had me when she was forty-one she is quite old now. It doesn't bother me much, but it bothers her. She's shaving her armpits now. What a palaver. I don't have any pubic hair yet, as I am small for my age – my heart wants me to be small, so it doesn't have to work too hard.

'Mum, can I help unpack something today?'

'Yeah, why not? We'll have a look in some of the smaller boxes from Grandma's.'

Grandma was small and plump and she knitted and sewed, tatted, smocked and embroidered. You never saw her without something in her hands that she was working on. Their garden was a fruit bowl of gooseberries and blackcurrants, redcurrants and raspberries, loganberries and strawberries. I used to throw a tennis ball up onto the roof of their bungalow and catch it when it bounced off the gutter. Another game with the ball was to roll it along the wavy low brick wall, which went around the front garden, and see how far it would go before it fell off. I got quite good at that.

They lived in Shoeburyness, quite close to London, where we lived when we were still a family, before Daddy left.

Like me, he's an only child. His parents, who I never met, came from this town.

Mum doesn't have any brothers or sisters either, so I have no aunts, uncles or cousins on her side of the family. There's only Mum now. Except that we are called Stevens and there are at least a hundred Stevenses in St Ives. I am determined to find my lost Cornish family, somehow.

Daddy isn't being at all helpful. He keeps saying he'll let me have his family tree, but he hasn't even given me a leaf yet. Mum is being positively obstructive: she doesn't want anything to do with Daddy's family and assumes they won't want anything to do with us. Anything Daddy related is a no-no. She has the screaming abdabs if I even mention him.

There's a wildlife warden we met out at Peregrine Cottage – the house we rented on the cliff – who said she has some relations called Stevens, but I've sort of lost touch with her since we moved. Ginnie.

It's sad how people drift in and out of our lives. Like my London friend Summer. I call her my friend, but I haven't seen her since we came to Cornwall. Maybe now we're settled in our own house, she will come and stay during school holidays. Or maybe I'll never see her again.

I don't suppose I'll ever see Shoeburyness again. Or smell the smell of it: cockle shells and seaweed and mud. The tide comes in very fast from a long way out, where the longest pier in the world ends. The water is a muddy brown colour though, not like the clear blue-green of St Ives. But there were wooden breakwaters to climb and balance on and I liked the pebbly beach, and finding white quartz stones to rub together to make a spark. Illuminations and neon lights shone all along the Golden Mile at Southend, where we bought fish and chips. Under the arches of a bridge there's a row of cafés with striped awnings and plastic tables and chairs set out on the pavement. Cafés with nautical names like The Mermaid, The Barge, Captain's Table. That was where I had my first experiences of eating out: sausage and mash or egg and chips, always with a cup of tea.

Grandpop and Grandma would take me to the pebbly beach and they'd hire deckchairs and we'd have fish-paste sandwiches and apples for tea. I could still run and climb then, and I would jump from roof to roof of the beach huts. (The beach huts had names too: *Sunny Days, Happy Days, Cosy Corner, Chez Nous*. That's French for *Our House*.)

Grandma was scandalised and tried to stop me, but

Grandpop would cheer me on.

'You can do it, princess.'

I don't look like a princess. I am small for my age and skinny and my skin is rather mauvish, I think. My hair Mum calls dark blonde, but to be honest it's mouse. 'Nothing Wrong with Mouse.'

'Oh, the elephants!' I unpack a troupe of elephants, three of them, each one a bit bigger than the one before, all with turned up ivory tusks and mother of pearl toes. I remember them standing on a window ledge. They are made of some heavy black wood, and carved. Looking closely, I see that they are slightly damaged – a piece of ear gone here, a tusk there. I remember them as being perfect, and Grandma saying, 'Be careful, my love.' I used to invent journeys for them across Africa, searching for greener pastures. I imagined them as a family – father, mother and baby. That was before I learned that the bull elephant doesn't hang around to bring up his baby. The mother has to do that on her own.

There's a pink-brown stone Buddha too, which I always loved to hold as it felt cold even on the hottest day, as if it contained something otherworldly. It has a smiling face, as if this god has a sense of humour. You don't get that impression about Jesus or God.

'Where shall we put them, Mum?'

'Have them in your room if you want.'

I put them on the stairs so I can carry them up next time I climb to my attic room. There are little piles of towels and sheets, clothes and books there already, waiting to be carried to their homes, like travellers in family groups at a bus station.

Grandpop travelled all over the world when he was in the Royal Navy and brought back lots of exotic souvenirs. We unpack a Japanese tea set they used to keep safe in a glass cabinet, thin porcelain coloured red and gold with little figures and landscapes.

'We'll use these,' Mum says.

'But aren't they terribly precious and worth lots of money?'

'No, it's only Japanese export stuff. We should enjoy them. What's the point of having pretty things gathering dust?'

Mum's good about stuff like that. She never makes a fuss if I break something. They're Only Things and Accidents Happen. I pick up a cup and look through it at the sun shining. It's a lovely thing.

'No dishwasher for these, Gussie, you'll have to wash them by hand.'

'No probs, Mum.' I am learning how to speak Strine – Australian – for when and if my new friend Brett comes to see me. No Worries. Crikey.

Mum sleeps in the main bedroom, the master bedroom, or I suppose it should be called the mistress bedroom, on the floor below me. There's a big bay window and the same view that I have, but slightly lower of course. The terrace faces south, there's plenty of sunshine all day long, and there's a little slab of concrete along the front path that gets the last of the sun. We sit there together on cushions and she drinks her whisky and I have a freshly squeezed orange juice or elderflower juice and we talk.

I think we talk more easily because we are not looking at each other. It's as if we are in a car, sitting next to each other, but looking ahead, and it's easier to say important things if you are not looking into each other's eyes. We have our eyes closed, because the sun is still so bright, and it's as if we are in a dream. I feel close to Mum when we talk like that.

'Don't you still love Daddy just a little bit?' I sometimes ask.

'No I bloody don't. He slept with other women. Why should I love him?'

'Okay, okay. I only asked.'

'I still feel very hurt, Gussie. Bastard! He betrayed me – us. He betrayed us.'

'Yeah, but if he wanted you to forgive him and he wanted to be with us, here, now, what would you say?'

'Fuck off, probably.' She sniffs. 'Anyway, we're okay on our own, aren't we?'

'I suppose.'

CHAPTER TWO

MUM HAS GONE out for the evening with Dr Dobbs – Alistair.

I'm playing Scrabble with Mrs Lorn. She is letting me win without much of a fight. Also I keep getting good letters – the high scoring C, Q and X so far. I put down all my letters straight away – QUIXOTIC, how about that! That's got to be the best score I've ever had. Probably the best score anyone has ever had in the entire history of Scrabble – 72, as it was on a double word score, plus 50 for putting down all my letters at once. She's getting all the rubbish, lots of vowels. She calls me 'my girl' with an extra 'r' in girl. Mrs Lorn has this habit of whistling when she's thinking – hymns, mostly. Sometimes she breaks into song. I do like Scrabble. I wish I wasn't winning so easily though. She's so old, she has probably given up the idea of winning.

'How old are you, Mrs Lorn?'

'As old as my feet but younger than my teeth and hair.'

She cackles like an old witch. 'Anyway, my girl, don't you know it's bad manners to ask a lady her age?'

'Why is it? Mum says she's fifty-two but her tits are only thirty-nine.'

Mrs Lorn screams with shocked laughter.

I like old people, apart from when they hug me or do that thing with my lips, you know, pinch them together so your mouth is an O and they make you say 'Sausages'. Though no one's done that to me for years. It's a torture aimed solely at small children who can't defend themselves. Like when they pull off your nose and show it to you and put it back again before you realise it's only their thumb and your nose is still where it always was, in the middle of your face. You've got to be very young to believe that. When you get to five it's too late, except for Father Christmas and fairies.

When I was three I can remember sitting at the window on Christmas Eve and I saw Father Christmas's sleigh pulled by reindeer in the sky. I really believed I saw it.

It must be wonderful to grow old like Mrs Lorn and know so much and have experienced a lot of life. It must make you wise if you can remember all those things you have heard and seen and read.

There's a old man who has three retriever dogs on leads accompanying him as he braves the roads at Carbis Bay in his electric wheelchair. He looks very heroic, as if he's in a horse-drawn chariot or on a dog sledge. I haven't seen him for a while, not since we left the cottage. We used to wave to him from the car but he didn't wave back. Probably he isn't able to. I wonder what he knows, and what he used to be before he became lopsided? And another very old man, always dressed immaculately in tweed suit and pork pie hat, straw hat in summer (Mr Dapper we call him), walks with the help of a stick all the way from Carbis Bay to St Ives and back each morning along the main road. He looks sad. Lonely. He's a guest at an old people's home.

Why do they put old people's homes in out of the way places? If I were old I would want to be in the middle of things, not on the outside ready to be shoved out of life when the time came. I suppose that's what I felt like when I was in the wilderness out at the cottage on the cliff. Apart from society. An outcast, cast away. Here in St Ives there's human life all around me.

Mum and Alistair have come back and he's off again, giving Mrs Lorn a lift home. She was delighted.

Mum looks flushed and smells of cigarettes and whisky and other people's beer. Her hair looks good. Her skirt's a bit short though. She must like him a lot.

Alistair's not half as handsome as Daddy. Daddy looks like a cross between Keanu Reeves and Bob Geldof, but not as scruffy as Bob Geldof. Alistair looks like a Dobbin horse, with his big ears and long face and nose. But he has kind eyes and a nice smile and always wears interesting ties. It must be difficult being a man and having to wear boring suits to work. I suppose a tie is one item you can decorate yourself with.

Like the bower bird. I think they attract females by making their nests, or bowers, look interesting.

'Bed, Gussie, Bed. Off You Go, Late. Late. Late.'

'Where did you go, Mum? Did you have a good time?'

'Sloop Inn. Fun, it was fun.'

'Did you meet anyone?'

'Alistair knows everyone.'

'Might he know Dad's relations, do you think?'

'Gussie. It's not the sort of thing you ask a man the first time he takes you out. You ask him. I'm going to bed, and You Should Too. Tired. You Look Tired.'

'Okay, okay, I'm going.'

I take my time getting upstairs, stop halfway to stroke Flo, who is on guard on the landing. She is such a school prefect, always keeping the other two cats in order, on their toes. I would be too, in their shoes. On their toes, in their shoes... interesting, these foot metaphors or whatever. Standing up for your beliefs. Filling his shoes. Knocking the socks off... Language is interesting.

I'd like to go to a school where they teach Latin, so I could study the roots of words. The local school is good apparently, but doesn't have Latin. I'll have to teach myself if I really want to learn. There was a *Winnie the Pooh* in Latin at our last house. *Winnie ille Pu.*

Lucus Lucubris Joris is Eeyore's Gloomy Place, which is *tristis et palustris*, rather boggy and sad.

Locus inondatus – floody place.

Domus mea – my house.

What about this one! *Fovea insidiosa ad heffalumpus catandos idonea* (Pooh trap for heffalumps).

I wrote those down so I could remember them. They were on the maps at both ends of the book. I like maps. There are lovely maps on the end pages of the Swallows and Amazons books too.

Mum said she entered her O-level German oral exam only knowing two phrases. One of them was – *Ich erkannte ihn an seinem Bart* – I recognised him by his beard. And the other phrase was – *Ich muss nach Hause gehen* – I must go home now. She managed to incorporate both into her conversation, and charmed the examiner with her knowledge of art – there was a Pieter Brueghel print to talk about. She spoke in English for most of the time and still passed.

I don't believe everything she tells me. She's a dreadful exaggerator.

Mum potters about downstairs, filling the dishwasher and putting the washing in the drier. Then she comes up too, carrying her hot water bottle. She feels the cold almost as much as me.

It's comforting having her in the room below, moving about, snoring in her sleep.

Our gulls are settled on the roof, hunkered down for the night, their heads tucked under their wings. There's no moon tonight and it's very cloudy. The wind is coming from the back of the house, the west, so I can open the front window without it rattling.

Tomorrow I'll go to the library and look for poetry books. There were loads at our last place.

I wonder if I'll ever meet Mr Writer – that's my name for the man who owns Peregrine Cottage. Maybe he's a murderer doing time. Or a famous poet on a world tour. He could be a bank manager, or a drug dealer, or a gunrunner. So many possibilities. Does anyone ever want to grow up to be a gunrunner or a car park attendant or a dinner lady?

I always wanted to be a cowboy until I realised, because I was a girl I could never ever be a cow*boy*. I was devastated that God had done this to me. It wasn't fair.

It didn't stop me dressing as a boy for quite a while afterwards though. I felt I had to gradually dissolve my boyhood and think myself slowly into being a girl. It wasn't easy.

I find it hard to go to sleep sometimes. I feel it's a waste of time, sleeping, when I could be reading or living. But then, dreaming is a sort of living, I suppose. I often have an exciting time in my dreams, more so than in my ordinary life. Sometimes in the middle of a dream one of the cats wakes me (chasing and killing something usually) and I get frustrated by the interruption. I usually forget an interrupted dream. Why is it so difficult to remember dreams? I feel cheated if I can't remember what happened.

Last night there were two birds. One was a little white owl sitting quietly on top of the book shelf in my room. The other was a miniature rail, buff and apricot coloured with black sharp beak, black legs and wide spread long black toes. It became scarlet and emerald, and stepped carefully across my books, as if they were water lily leaves. I think there is a bird called a Jesus bird – because it looks like it's walking on water. It might have been one of those.

My own room: I do like it. All my babyhood is on the top shelf of the large book case: faded and worn Teddy, who has never had another name; Panda, from a trip Daddy made to Germany; Nightie Dog, that used to be Mum's and has a zip in its tummy for pyjamas; several knitted toys, including Noddy, that Grandma made for me. He's very old and his colours have faded but his bell still rings on the end of his night cap. And Rena Wooflie, my favourite, a soft stuffed girl dog with checked dress and apron. Mum bought her for me in Mombasa the very first time we went to Africa, because I had lost my cuddly comfort blanket on the journey.

I love Rena Wooflie and she has to come with me to hospital. It's for her sake, not mine. She gets lonely, as she doesn't talk the same language as Panda or Teddy or Nightie Dog. Rena Wooflie and I speak Swahili together.

jambo – hello
abari? – how are you?
msuri – good
paka – cat
malaika – angel
kuku – fowl
simba – lion
nyuki – bee
kidege – a little bird
kufa tutakufa wote – as for dying, we shall all die.

That's all I know really but I do still have a phrase book so I could in theory learn some more.

That first winter in Africa there was a family with a little boy about my age – three – and he was desperate for my Rena Wooflie. No matter that he had hundreds of teddies and soft toys, he wanted my one and only. My mum bought another one and gave it to him. Its head wasn't at quite the same angle as my Rena Wooflie's and he started to moan and grizzle, and he threw it and yelled, and his mother picked it up and yanked its head around and said – Is that better? And I could tell she was pretending it was her little boy's head she was twisting, not the toy's.

I would never abuse my Rena Wooflie.

On top of my wardrobe, looking down at me is Horsey. He was my baby walker, a horse on wheels. Mum tried to throw him away once because the metal neck pole had pushed through the straw and fur and his head was in danger of coming off. She placed Horsey by the dustbins the day before dustbin day, and then it started to rain so she brought him in again. That was years ago. He's still here, mended of course with a new patch of different coloured fake fur. He's part of the family now.

Noah's Ark completes childhood on the high shelf. It was Mum's when she was little. There are pairs of little wooden hand-painted lions and elephants, sheep and cows, hippos and zebra, and I've added other tiny animals found over the years – a lead crocodile, a glass cat, a wooden cat, and my favourite, a giraffe made of bone.

CHAPTER THREE

MORNINGS IN MID September smell fresher than August, and there's lots of swirling white mist over the water, hiding the dunes and estuary. But the air is still and somehow you know it's going to be sunny later. The heavy band of mist is chrome and silver; the clouds are the colour of lavender leaves and steamed up mirrors. The sea is hammered pewter and the low waves are mercury creeping up the beach. Where the sun breaks through, it explodes on the water in a firework burst of sparkling stars. On the other side of the bay, battleship clouds float above the dunes and hills of Gwithian and Godrevy.

September is like a wonderful monochrome photograph or the opening credits of an obscure French movie. Like the ones Daddy used to take me to.

Yesterday evening we went to Porthmeor Beach to see the really high tide. Waves clapped like thunder on the walls of the studios and apartments on the beach and rolled up and over in a constant tumult. We hung over the wall with lots of other people and watched boys and girls run along the top of the sand racing the waves and getting soaked. Most of the tourists had gone home to get ready for dinner.

It was as if the holidaymakers had been swept away and the sand wiped clean of summer. The Island (which isn't really an island but that's what it's called) turned from green to orange in the setting sun. It has a little chapel on the top and reminds me of the Paula Rega painting – *The Dance*. Maybe it isn't a painting. She did huge pastel drawings. Mum has loads of books on painters and we've unpacked some already.

Our new house in St Ives is not new new, it's Victorian

– a terraced house on three floors. I love having the attic room – I know it's crazy for me to want to climb all these stairs, but it's worth it for the view: right over the grey and orange roofs down to the harbour and across the bay to the lighthouse and beyond.

I have a white painted cast iron bed and a new quilt, pink and blue cotton stripes and roses. I chose it from a catalogue. It's very girlie. Not my usual style at all.

The ceiling slopes to the roof and I have a real watercolour painting on the wall, which shows almost the same scene I see from the window but from a slightly different angle. The walls and ceiling are white and I have white cotton curtains. When the light changes, as it does all the time, the room turns blue or pink or pale green or mauve. A small roof window sheds a square of light on my bed.

On my chest of drawers there's a photograph of Grandpop and Grandma made by Daddy. There's also a photograph of Daddy and Mum getting married that Mum won't have in her room, so I've got it. I think it's because she doesn't want to be reminded of how happy they were together. And there's a photograph of our three cats lying on a sofa together – a rare event.

We are just far enough away from the main streets not to hear the holidaymakers, though we do hear the fishing trip boatman calling out over his loud speaker. 'Seal Island. Boat leaving in ten minutes for Seal Island.'

We are close enough to get to the shops and beaches very easily. Getting back up again is another story. But I can see people coming up the hill from my window. People! It's wonderful to be near people again. I had begun to talk to myself at Peregrine Cottage, or anyway, to the cats. There were no people to talk to out on the cliff.

I don't count Mum of course. She's not terribly good at talking to me, except to tell me what not to do – Don't

Overdo it, Don't go for Walks along the Cliff, Don't Wear that Hat – that sort of thing. I was quite ill before we left, and she was really worried about me. I think she's happier too, now we are in the town.

I miss the badgers coming to the kitchen door for peanuts at night, and the sight of gannets folding back their wings and plunging like arrows into the sea just off the point. I miss the crickets climbing up the wooden walls, and the slowworms, which would appear mysteriously on the sitting room floor or on the doormat.

I expect the cats will soon forget all those dear little harvest mice and voles they used to kill. At least the wildlife population will increase, now the cats have left.

I hope the robins and blue-tits and greenfinches will survive the coming winter without us feeding them sunflower seeds. Maybe the owner will return from wherever he has been all these months.

Up on the cliffs we could hear oystercatchers and curlews calling to each other.

Herring gulls nest on the roof here. Or rather, they were nesting earlier in the year, and their one chick is making the most mournful noise imaginable. He hunches his shoulders so his neck disappears and he makes this awful rasping noise. I want to give him an inhaler. He keeps nearly sliding off the roof, and it's a long drop to the garden or to the little lane behind the house. He's flapping his speckled wings and jumping up and down, trying to copy all the other gulls that are circling the town, screaming and chuckling and murmuring to each other. They are very sociable creatures. It's wonderful to see and hear so many of them. There's even a pair of Great Black-backed gulls on a roof nearby.

Every roof of the little town has its own gull family who tuck themselves into valley-gutters or next to chimneys, out of the wind. They are good parents, feeding their young even when they are as big as they are and making this horrible racket. The mother or father bird lands on the roof and the chick immediately goes up to it and starts pecking at the scarlet spot on the beak. The parent eventually throws up – that's what it looks like – regurgitates the food for the young bird to eat.

It's wonderful to be on the same level as the nesting birds and to watch their everyday life. The male is larger and more powerful looking than the female herring gull, but they both have a vast vocabulary. They seem to communicate in all sorts of ways. They have a companionable chuckling call, a loud angry screech, a mewing, sad, lonely call and sometimes you hear them grumbling to themselves while flying. Our parent gulls get really angry and throw their heads back and scream a warning if others try to land on the same roof.

Most of them have left the summer nests on the roofs now, but our gulls have to hang around a while longer until their offspring has learned to fly. He must have been a late summer baby.

Like me.

Mum is unpacking our stuff from London that never got unpacked at our rented place. She insists I rest every afternoon, so that's why I am up here and she is downstairs. I can hear her singing. She must be feeling happy. I hope so.

Mrs Lorn is helping out with washing the crockery. There are newspaper words over every plate and cup. I think we should leave them like that to make mealtimes more interesting but Mum insists they are washed. Mrs Lorn is whistling loudly, like she does. We sort of inherited her from Peregrine Cottage. She's Mr Lorn's wife: he was the gardener there. We don't need a gardener here. The garden is Not Big Enough to Swing a Cat in, but there's a washing line and a little square of grass, and a pretty fence that looks like it should be metal but it's wooden. The wooden gate (which also looks like it's made of metal) opens onto a path, which goes along the front of this terrace and reaches a dead end after number nine. We look down over a steep little hill over the harbour and town. I think it's perfect.

Mum bought the house while I was being ill. She had been looking for months for the right property in St Ives. I was desperate to get into the town so I could make friends and get about more. I am quite recovered now. Or rather, I'm feeling much better than I was a few weeks ago.

Actually, I am waiting for a heart and lung transplant. I can still get around, more or less, but I get very out of breath and go rather bluer than normal. Not that it's normal to be blue, just normal for me. The hill is a challenge, but there's an old bench halfway up, and I can always sit on the steps when I need to.

I now have a special bleeper thingy too, in case the hospital finds a donor for me. Someone is going to have to die for me to get a chance at living longer, but I try not to think too much about the stranger whose organs will be inside me, pumping my blood and my breath around my body.

One Step at a Time.

When you think about it, there's no such thing as the future. We only assume there is. There is now, this second, and the remembered past.

The past is important to me. I have done many interesting things in my life, so I have some good memories. But the future? There's no such thing. There's only today. Live for Today is my motto. Mine and Mum's. Every moment I have now is precious.

To get back to my room – Flo, Charlie and Rambo have already sussed out that this is where I spend most of my time and they've made it their base. Flo is curled up on a cushion on a wicker chair, Rambo is trying to look like a Trafalgar Square lion on the floor in a patch of sun and succeeding rather well and Charlie is of course, on my lap as per usual. They didn't approve of being moved in small cramped baskets from Peregrine Cottage to here, but it was only ten minutes at the most in the car. Rambo shat himself though. Poor cat. He is always car sick and terrified of anything and everything. Mum had to wash his bottom.

The cats spent the first week under my bed. I had to feed them up here, placing their food and bowl of water close by. We put Rambo's litter box on the front door mat for all of them to use, but I'm afraid there have been one or two little presents on the doormat itself. I expect the two females consider the box as Rambo territory and won't use it.

Flo was the first to venture forth and discover the delights of 5 Bowling Green: stairs, cupboards, carpet smells, high shelves. Flo likes high shelves. She is the only one of the cats who looks around her *and* above her. She is like a detective, determined to investigate every possible hiding place, or way out, more like. She hates to be enclosed. She has to find an escape route. Maybe she has claustrophobia. I reckon she is the most intelligent of the three cats. I love Charlie of the green eyes, but I have to admit that she is not terribly bright.

And Flo is the only one who likes playing games with me, especially in the morning, after breakfast, sometimes instead of breakfast. Her favourite toy is the plastic ring that comes off the top of a plastic milk carton. She'll pretend it's a mouse and throw it and chase it and catch it and kill it. She has a vivid imagination. The others look on with complete disdain – or incomprehension. She is not at all embarrassed. She just enjoys life, Flo, and I admire her. She plays catch and football with me, pushing the toy to me and when I throw it to her she sends it back.

She reminds me of my Grandma. Grandma played cricket and she was always going to dances, and she used to dance with other old women, can you imagine? I would die rather than dance with another girl, if I had the chance to dance with a boy. Not that I've ever been dancing. If you think about it it's a very strange thing to do. I can understand the ritual bit about attracting a partner – the highest jumping dancer in the Masai tribe, I think it is, for instance. But why do old people do it? Apart from getting physical exercise I can't see the reason for it, unless it's a widow or widower looking for another mate.

Some birds have complicated dance rituals, I know. The male great bustard throws back his wings and head, apparently turning his head inside out.

Grandpop didn't go in for dancing. He obviously diddn't feel the need to keep attracting Grandma.

I miss them very much. They were the best grandparents. Grandpop died last year when I was in hospital having an operation and Grandma died a few days later, of a broken heart. I was eleven.

I remember them sitting on their old green sofa, watching telly, holding hands.

Like boy and girl sweethearts, holding hands. Grandpop's faded tattoos on his arms, the sleeves of his white collarless shirt folded up, elasticated silver bands above his elbows. He had an old rocking chair and when I was little I sat on his lap and we rocked together. He smelt of tobacco. Sometimes he had a little patch of cigarette paper, *Rizla* paper it was called, very thin like tissue paper, stuck to some part of his face – his cheek or chin, where he cut himself shaving. And he usually had a cigarette tucked behind one ear – for later. He rolled his own cigarettes and taught me how to do it, though obviously, I haven't ever told Mum.

Of course, I would never ever smoke anyway, with my heart. I don't really understand how anyone can inhale stuff that's going to make them breathless and possibly cause cancers all over their body. Perhaps if human beings had evolved to be transparent so we could see exactly what was going on inside of us, we wouldn't eat fatty things that clog up our arteries, or take drugs that destroy our brains, or drink and smoke too much. Or maybe we would be fascinated by the sight of smoke whirling around in our lungs and keep on doing it.

I would love not to be breathless. I do remember what it felt like to be able to run and climb and play physical games and, best of all, to swim and snorkel. But I haven't been able to do any of that stuff for a few years now. Not since my heart had to work extra hard to keep me alive. When I was little I was pretty normal, I think. Well, it felt normal.

I have something called Pulmonary Atresia – a rare congenital disease, and people who have it usually die when they are very young. But I have been lucky. There are other defects in my heart muscle, but my blood does get oxygenated to a certain extent, so I am still alive. As I get bigger my heart won't be able to cope with the extra work and I'll need that operation.

'Mum, Mu-um, Mu-uum!'

The whistling and singing stops.

'What?'

'What happened to Grandpop's rocking chair?'

'I gave it to his cricket club.'

'Oh. And why didn't you save it for me?'

'Gussie, I Refuse to Shout,' she shouts.

I wonder who is sitting in it now? Has it an inscription of Grandpop's name? Do little boys fight to rock in it? I hope no one has burned cigarette holes in the upholstery.

Grandma used to hang a clean antimacassar – that's a sort of lacy or embroidered cloth – over the back. I bet no one at the cricket club thinks to do that. It will get stained from greasy heads, like all those chairs in the hospital waiting room. The thought of his favourite chair being abused depresses me.

To get back to my cats: Rambo is the least brave of the three. He looks wonderfully royal and proud and courageous until someone stands up. Then he runs and hides. He cowers. He's a coward and scared of Flo, with good reason. She is fierce and fearsome, fearless and feisty, and I am sorry to say – a bully. I think she just can't stand the fact that the other two are such wusses. She has no patience. I do love her though. She has guts, chutzpah, presence. She is definitely the matriarch, the alpha female, the boss, queen bee, big momma, top cat.

The first day here I rubbed butter on their paws – the usual procedure to make them want to be where we are, and gave them lots of goodies – Parmesan cheese, curried chicken, that sort of thing. But cats hate change. They haven't been allowed outside yet. We have to find someone to put a cat-flap in the front door first. I've seen other cats around, so they'll have to meet them and sort out territorial rights.

The little cobbled lanes and alleyways and steps of Downlong are full of cats. Black cats, grey cats, orange cats, tabby cats, fat cats and slender cats. There's a weird looking cat that sits in a window in Back Road West. It has hardly any hair. It is a pink and grey colour with enormous ears. Hideous.

I haven't let our cats see inside the deep dark cupboards under the eaves yet. I'm afraid they might find a way out. As it is they sit on the window ledge and do that chittering thing cats do with their mouths as if they are freezing cold when they see birds and want to eat them. It's as if they can't help it, their teeth just start rattling fast in anticipation of the feast. Or maybe they are swearing, saying disgusting things in catspeak, threatening a horrible death by a thousand bites and claw stabs.

CHAPTER FOUR

MUM IS IN the garden fixing up a bird feeder. It's a sort of metal tree – a tall thin metal trunk with two curved branches turning up at the ends so you can hang bird feeders on it. We've bought a bag of peanuts and a bag of black sunflower seeds.

Our little front garden, although it is so small, will be part of a long green corridor of plants, trees and seed heads, home for insects, worms and caterpillars. The terrace is nearly forty houses long, if you take into account the other front gardens further up the hill, so the little birds have a good supply of food and cover.

I'm sitting on the doorstep on a cushion in the sun and the three cats are sitting behind me, staring at their new minuscule garden. I get up and walk six steps across the patch of grass to Mum, taking her the seeds.

Flo is of course the first to follow me into darkest unknown territory. She is so brave. Charlie follows her, crouched low, on the lookout for danger, but Rambo isn't going anywhere. He skulks in the passage, his nose twitching suspiciously. The two females sniff every blade of grass to see who has been here before them. Flo opens her mouth and goes Ugh! I laugh at her. She is suitably embarrassed and runs inside and up the stairs, terrifying Rambo, who tears off into the kitchen. Only Charlie remains in the garden. She has gone under the wooden garden seat and is sniffing at a bag of potting compost. I crouch down with her and peer into the bag.

'Oh Mum, look, a toad.'

Mum is hammering the metal tree as hard as she can into the earth. She likes toads too.

'We could have a tiny pond if you like.'

'Yeah, great! Tadpoles. We can have tadpoles.'

'We could have goldfish.'

'We can't have goldfish, Mum. They eat tadpoles.'

'Do they?'

'Yes, they do.' Honestly, why is she so ignorant?

It occurs to me that tropical fish have a hard time in films, especially in action movies. If there's a huge fish tank with lots of colourful fish swimming around – Oho – you know they'll soon be floundering on the floor with broken glass, water gushing everywhere, gunshots, blood and guts. You know that bit at the end of the film when they give the credits, and it says: 'No animals were harmed in the making of this film.' It doesn't mention fish, does it? It's gratuitous violence, that's what it is.

I've started a list of movies where fish tanks get smashed:

1. *Arabesque*
2. *Lethal Weapon 2*
3. In another movie a convict smashed a polythene bag with a goldfish in but I can't remember the title. The climax had the heroes finding diamonds among the rocks of the fish collector's aquarium.
4. *A Fish Called Wanda* – Maybe the fish tank doesn't get smashed but the fish get eaten alive.

The bird feeder is great. We go indoors and leave the little birds to get used to their new metal tree. Charlie comes too. Flo and Charlie sit on the window seat of the living room to do some serious bird-watching.

'A young blue-tit is particularly tasty, Charlie, take note,' says Flo. 'You must leave the head though, it is rather tough and not worth the bother.'

There is a low stone 'hedge' between our house and the house next door with valerian and wild honeysuckle growing out of it. The door of the house is open onto a storm porch, that's a sort of small area between the front door and a coloured glass door. All these terraced houses were built with them, as a protection from the wind. Ours is particularly pretty with red squares in the corners, deep blue strips of glass around the sides and white opaque glass in the middle with an anchor engraved on it.

Our neighbour comes out in her apron and with a basket of washing. Her ginger cat follows her and she sits on the step with the cat pushing its head against her.

'Hello,' says Mum and we introduce ourselves. She's smiley, small and skinny, hunched over like I imagine Red Riding Hood's granny, with grey hair in a bun, and is called Mrs Thomas. Her cat is called Shandy. Mrs Thomas's apron is patterned with flowers the same colours as the valerian – pink and white and red. She hangs up huge white cotton knickers, vests and stockings and props up the line with a long pole. She's not Cornish, she tells us, she's from Devon, but she was married to a local man, who died two years ago, and she still misses him badly. She goes in and comes out straight away with a framed photograph of her husband, a lifeboatman. 'The love of my life,' she says.

I met TLOML when I was watching birds on the coast path at Peregrine Cottage. He's Australian. He has started at the local secondary school, as I would have done this term if I had been well enough. He came to see me when I was really sick, except that I wasn't well enough to see him. He's very unusual in that he isn't keen on sports and he actually thinks I am interesting. He's got floppy blond hair and a curly mouth and he too likes books. He's called Brett.

Desert Island Discs is on the radio. I think there should be a *Desert Island Books* where the guest tells us which eight books he/she would take.

I have started my list of favourite books for when I am

famous and invited on the programme:

Jennie by Paul Gallico
House at Pooh Corner by AA Milne
The Collected Short Stories of Katherine Mansfield
White Fang by Jack London
Middlemarch by George Eliot
Pride and Prejudice by Jane Austen
Catcher in the Rye by JD Salinger
Fabre's Book of Insects
Lord of the Flies by William Golding

That's nine and I'll only be allowed eight so I'll have to think about which one I could live without.

I would like to take a bird identification book with me, suitable for the region of the desert island, and some poems, but I don't know enough about poetry yet to decide which to take. Perhaps that should be my next self-education project. As long as I keep reading, I will know almost as much as if I was at school – except for maths. And I'd have the Bible and the complete works of Shakespeare of course. I haven't read either of those. What would I take for my luxury?

I would miss Charlie most of all. But I don't think pets are allowed on the desert island. I suppose an unending supply of paper and pencils would be best, then I could record what I see, keep a journal, and maybe write poems and stuff and draw pictures of the animals and flowers and birds. Presumably I would be cast away with my glasses intact. What they don't explain is how you are supposed to have got on the desert island. If there was a shipwreck you could swim out to it and gather useful stuff like rope and matches and candles and food, as Robinson Crusoe did. He even had a dog and cat and chickens. And there would be binoculars and maps and books, and crystal chandeliers and silver cutlery and the clothes of dead passengers. I could walk about in a ball gown and a captain's cap and live on caviar and champagne.

When we had winters in Africa we lived on coconuts and bananas, papayas and parrotfish. It was very like being on a desert island. Except we did have someone to help cook and clean. I wouldn't have to clean though, would I? Just sweep the woven palm leaf matting with a bundle of sticks tied together to make a broom. I would be rather good at living on my own. I could tame a parrot and a monkey or find an orphaned bush baby or something – another living creature to talk to.

CHAPTER FIVE

IT HAS TAKEN four days for the little birds to get used to our metal tree. I got Mum to move it further into the flowerbed so the trunk is more hidden in the middle of a bush and the birds have cover. They like to hide quickly after they have fed and when they are queuing for their turn to stand on the feeder. Greenfinches are the most numerous and greedy. They love peanuts and sunflower seeds. But there's a pair of stunningly colourful goldfinches too, and starlings.

I like starlings. They aren't beautiful; they have large gawky heads and an awkward way of walking and they look like they have been knitted with black and white wool. When the sun hits them they have an oily, blue-green tinge, like fresh mackerel. They are extremely talkative and I like the clicketty click noise they make followed by a long falling whistle. Their language is more interesting and complicated than most birds'.

One stands on the telegraph line outside my window and whistles and clicks non-stop to the sky. I wonder what he's saying? Perhaps he's communing with his ancestors or giving thanks to the Sky-God for giving him life. Starlings walk around in Fore Street finding crumbs, totally ignored by the people ambling along, though I think the birds are just as interesting, if not more, than what's in the shop windows – surf boards, bikinis, framed pictures made of clock and watch parts.

I'm glad to say we have a resident robin. He grazes (can robins graze?) on the droppings from the feeders. Blue-tits and great-tits come too and even sparrows. (We had no sparrows or starlings at Peregrine Point.)

The cats have started to go outside. We still haven't got a

cat flap fitted, but we leave the front door open so they can go in and out when they want. It's amazing being able to leave the door open. You couldn't do that in Camden Town. You'd have North London dropouts squatting in half an hour and turning it into a den of iniquity with drug dealers queuing up outside and junkies shooting up and/or throwing up in the bushes.

Rambo doesn't go out. He sits on the doormat and watches the other two. He is such a wuss. Mum has to bring in his litter box at night because he's scared of the dark. He is sleeping on a cushion in the front window.

I think cats sleep so much because they are bored. They aren't the least bit creative so the ones that aren't fantasists like Flo sleep a lot. If you are creative you have a life of the imagination and you are forever occupied. But cats don't have that stuff. They are our pets; we feed them and keep them warm. They don't need to hunt for survival. Even sex has been removed from their lives as they've all been neutered or whatever. No wonder they're bored. No wonder they sleep so much.

It has rained all day, but the sun has made a brief appearance low in the sky and has turned the flying gulls' bellies pink and gold.

I am still making lists of the books I like best. *To Kill a Mockingbird* is good. The hero is the father, a lawyer. It is a story about a rape and he defends the accused black man. It is also the story of children growing up and facing their fears. Another good adventure is *High Wind in Jamaica* by Richard Hughes. It's got a murder in it and kidnapped children on a pirate ship. It starts with a terrifying hurricane and the terrible death of their pet, Tabby, torn apart by wild cats. I realise now on a second reading that I only imagined the actual death of Tabby. The writer of the story leaves the reader to fill in the untold horrors.

I'm having second thoughts on having *Lord of the Flies* on my island. It's about a large group of small boys on a desert island in war-time with no grown-ups. The boys soon become savages and start murdering each other. It's really scary. I think it might give me nightmares, so I'll leave it behind.

I'm lucky to have a vivid imagination – Mum would say it was a bad thing to have lots of – but it does mean that although I am sort of imprisoned in my less than perfect body, I am free to wander wherever I want to go in my mind.

CHAPTER SIX

HERE ARE SOME of the names of the little streets in the old town that Mum and I have just walked through: Court Cocking; Love Lane; Mount Zion; Salubrious Place; Teetotal Street; Virgin Street; Fish Street.

We're having lunch at a small beach café, sitting in the sunshine overlooking the dear little beach, which sits between the Island and the harbour.

Sparrows hop around under our feet looking for crumbs and even come on the table. The young ones fluff up their feathers and look pitiful so their parents will feed them. Two very handsome young starlings are less brave but are also enjoying our generosity. They already have black and white chests but their faces and heads and shoulders are still a pretty light brown colour. I can't see their parents anywhere so I suppose they are independent now. The adults have found an ideal place to leave their young – a restaurant where they can have free food three times a day. In winter, when the café closes, they'll join their friends in Fore Street and hang around outside the bakers.

Shopping in St Ives is much more interesting than going to a supermarket. We get really tasty bread and pasties in Fore Street or Tregenna Place, and the fresh fish shop in Back Road East is called Stevens – so we might be related. They have hake, haddock, mackerel, wild sea bass, mullet, megrim sole, gurnard, crabmeat, lobster, mussels, sardines, salmon, ling, scallops, prawns, any fish in season, all displayed beautifully on marble slabs with ice packed around them and chunks of lemon. As good as Harrods any day – better, as the fish is fresh from the sea, and Stevens is nearer to the sea than Harrods so the fish have the same postcode as the customers.

I used not to eat fish or meat or cheese or eggs or anything, Mum says, I only ate chips and nuts and ice cream. But I don't remember. She says it was because I was force-fed through a tube up my nose and down my throat for the first few months of my life and didn't associate food with love or enjoyment.

I do now. My favourite food is soup – the sort of soup that Mum cooks, with home-made stock and fresh vegetables.

This is Mum's recipe for French Onion Soup:

Make a stock from left over chicken and its carcase, onion and carrot, celery and any fresh herbs. (She also uses vegetable stock from when she cooks spinach, greens and potatoes or whatever.)

Cook several large sliced onions in butter until they have melted into a sticky goo.

Add the strained stock and cook for about 20 minutes.

Arrange sliced rounds of oven-toasted French bread in the bottom of a heavy casserole.

Sprinkle plenty of Gruyère cheese on top.

Pour some soup over the bread.

Add another layer of bread.

Sprinkle more cheese.

Add rest of soup.

Place in oven, uncovered, and cook for about 45 minutes or until the top is crusty and brown.

It isn't very liquid; it's a thick gluey soup and it's better the next day and even better if you pour a little red wine over the soup in the bowl. I am allowed to drink red wine if it's in the soup. French children do it all the time, Daddy says. He is a Francophile – which means he loves anything French.

Oh why is he so vague about his rellies? (Australian for

relations.) He did say he would send me a list of names of his second cousins twice removed or whatever, but he hasn't yet. He is always very busy; he works for a film archive in London and travels all over the place to film festivals. He used to be a photographer and filmmaker, but he hasn't had any films shown in cinemas. He gave me one of his old cameras – a Nikkormat. It's silver metal and black, rather heavy, but I like the weight of it. You can hold it steady and it doesn't shake when you press the button to take a picture.

I might start taking pictures of St Ives. I like all the old cottages and their little gardens. I could make a record of the way things are now. For posterity. Like the way people without gardens hang out their washing on the front of the house. The cats. I could photograph all the cats.

Daddy gave me a load of 35mm black and white 400 ASA slow film, which means I can take pictures in fairly dark situations, like indoors, without using a flash. I don't have a flash. I only use the 50 ml lens. It's too complicated to keep changing lenses, and anyway I can't carry a heavy bagful of stuff. Dad said to keep things simple. He says that most amateur photographers have too much equipment and don't care about the end product, only the hardware – boys' toys. He says you can make perfectly good images with a standard 50 ml lens. It's almost like the way you see things with your ordinary eyes.

Daddy made some lovely portraits of Grandpop and Grandma on their wedding anniversary the year before they died. I'm glad he did that. Daddy was good at getting people to relax and look natural in photographs.

Mum and Daddy took me to several photo exhibitions in London and I remember one in particular. It was an exhibition of work by a famous photographer called Kertesz, a Hungarian who lived in America. He used a 35 mm SLR camera and made lots of pictures taken from up high, looking down on street scenes or gardens. You *make* photographs, Daddy told me, you don't *take* them. Taking them sounds like stealing. He said, 'You must always try to ask people's permission before you make a picture of them, otherwise it is like theft.'

Life is interesting looking down on people and objects. They become foreshortened, and shadows are very important. Black and white photos accentuate the light and dark really well, much better than if you use colour.

I could do that looking onto the garden, except that not much happens down there and the birds would be almost invisible.

I lean out of my attic window and expose a few frames (take a few pictures) of our washing line. Sheets flap and soar as if they are dancing and make a slapping clapping sound. Actually, I'm not too good at heights, but looking through the viewfinder of a camera turns the experience into something quite different. It is a framed image, my own, not a vertigo episode. I can choose what goes into the picture and what stays out of it. I won't allow the telegraph pole and wire to become part of this picture, I crop them out as I focus. Then I make a picture of the starling on the wire, his throat exposed as he talks to the sky.

Oops! I nearly lost my cap out the window. Alistair gave it to me. It's a navy blue cotton cap with a crown and three lions on the front – an England cricket cap. I used to wear a battered trilby hat that Grandpop gave me. At first I wore it because I was little and being a cowboy and then I wore it because Grandpop died. Also it made me feel like Indiana Jones. He never lost his hat even when he was swimming. I lost mine in a gale. It flew into the sea and was never seen again. I do like hats.

Charlie is curled on the blue striped cushion. I do a close up of her. She has the advantage of being already black and white. She has one eye open, suspicious of my intent. The trouble with cats is, when you try to photograph them they walk straight towards you, so all you get is the narrow chest and head and the straight up tail. They are desperate for attention. Charlie yawns and stretches white paws towards me. Oh dear, I'll have to stroke her now. I can't resist her pretty paws.

Flo went through a strange patch a while ago, when I first had Charlie. She would stare through narrowed eyes at me stroking Charlie and when I went to stroke her she would run away. Then she started to scratch me when I walked past her, attacking with a sudden fury. It was very odd. I soon realised that she was missing my loving attention and showing her misery in the only way she knew. So from then on I've made a point of always making a big fuss of her before I stroke Charlie. Flo comes first, she must: she is the alpha female and knows her place. I had forgotten it for a while, but now I know better.

Seen from a distance, the roofs of St Ives look like they are covered in buttercup petals. I lean out the window again to study the mustard coloured lichens. Like miniature atolls, they grow into a circle, but the middle bits die and leave a ring, like orange rind. Some of them are flowering. If you look at them closely through a lens it's like snorkelling over coral.

I did so love that: snorkelling in Africa. It was the best time ever. I'll never forget it. Everything about being there was interesting. There were huge millipedes like miniature tube trains. I'd place them on my arms and watch them move slowly up to my shoulder. Mum shuddered when I did that. And the pretty blue and yellow spotted lizards that ate the mosquitoes. They lived on the outside walls and inside the house – Pelican Cottage.

It's funny how we've lived in places with bird names.

Maybe we could give this house a bird name? Starling's Nest; Seagull House; Gull's Nest; Gull Rock; Goldfinch Gulch; Robin's Rest; Finch's Folly. Number 5 sounds so boring.

We had cockroaches in Africa. Mum wasn't at all keen on those. A pair lived under my bed and I wouldn't let her throw them out. After all, they were there before we were. It's their country. I fed them breadcrumbs. They made friendly scuttling sounds all night. Outside there were enormous butterflies and praying mantises and beetles so big they sounded like flying mopeds. My favourite thing was exploring the reef at low tide, discovering all the sea margin life; shellfish, starfish, anemones, sea cucumbers, crabs.

I'll be able to do that here. There are rock pools on several of the beaches – Porthmeor, by the Island; Porthgwidden; the little beach by the museum – I don't know what it's called. And on Porthminster Beach and Carbis Bay there are lots.

Where we were at Peregrine Point there were caves and pools but the climb was steep so I wasn't up to exploring much. We used to gather mussels though, and Mum cooked them with chopped onion and white wine. You have to clean them thoroughly in clean running water for a while, or stick them somewhere cold in clean water until you need them.

They look disgusting – like the insides of a squashed hedgehog – but close your eyes and they taste like the smell of the sea.

Mrs Thomas is in her attic room too. She is opening the window and putting out bread for the gulls. Perhaps she thinks the male is the spirit of her dead husband. She waves when she sees me. If Mum is right and all seamen come back as seagulls there must be dozens of widows and bereaved mothers all over St Ives, Mousehole and Newlyn and other seaside towns looking after their own personal family gulls.

It must be difficult to carry on living when everyone you love is dead.

CHAPTER SEVEN

IF I HAD been born a hundred years ago I wouldn't have survived a week, even. Without antibiotics, and digitalis – a heart drug that comes from the foxglove – I would have died in babyhood. Without transplantation expertise and organ donation I wouldn't have any hope of living much longer. I'm lucky to have been born in the twentieth century.

We are picnicking on my favourite beach, Porthmeor, sitting up against the granite wall below the artists' studios, facing the big rollers dashing in and the low sun. It's still warm enough to wear a T-shirt. There are quite a few holidaymakers here, tanned from a week of sunshine. We are sitting close to a ladder that goes from the sand up to the door of a beach house. A group of people sit drinking white wine and beer and passing a big bag of crisps between them. There are some wrinklies and two babies and three toddlers and several older children too, who are running around giving the little ones towel rides on the sand.

Most people on this beach are hiding behind windbreaks but not this crowd.

'Gussie, don't stare. It's rude.'

'I'm not.'

'You are.'

I am. I do that. It's a bad habit. But I am genuinely interested in other people. It's like being an anthropologist studying the behaviour of a lost tribe. I can't help it. Better than being totally uninterested in life around me.

At Peregrine Cottage there was only Nature to observe. Here, there's loads of people. There's a rather lovely woman, tall and slender, dark, who is holding a tiny baby, not hers. She has a sweet face, not exactly pretty, but more than pretty, glowing and kind – concerned. Her husband is much older and wrinkly and very tanned. He is obviously well known, like a Godfather figure. People keep making a detour to come to him as they are walking along the beach. They don't kiss his ring or his hand though. They sit for a while and are offered a glass of wine or a little bottle of beer.

'He must know everybody. I wonder if he knows Daddy's family?'

'Gussie, stop it!'

'What?'

'You know what. Don't Do it!'

'Oh look Mum!' The weird, big-eared cat is standing at the top of the ladder looking down at his family on the beach. One of the girls climbs the ladder and carries the cat down. She places it on a rug and strokes it.

I yearn to go and say hello, but I am suddenly shy. Why? In the past I would be perfectly able to meet new people. Am I too grown up to be naturally gregarious and sociable? I make myself stand and walk slowly to where the cat is. I crouch to look at him.

'Hello, may I stroke him?'

The child, who is like a little fairy, with fine blonde hair and white skin, nods at me, and I reach out to touch the strange creature. His back is barely covered with a fine curly down, hardly fur, more like velvet or felt, and he has no eyebrows or fur on his face. His pink belly is loose and swings from his ribs when he moves.

'He feels strange,' I say. 'What is he called?

'Wobert, he's a Sphinx, a throwback,' says the little girl, 'but he's very clever. He carries his blanket around.'

Poor little cat. His eyes bulge, his ears are huge, he looks and feels so weird, sweaty skinned, warm and clammy, I bet he doesn't get stroked or cuddled much.

'I have to take him in now, or he'll get sunburned.' She

lifts him carefully and takes him up the ladder.

There are too many Stevenses in this town. I looked them up in the local telephone directory: two fish merchants, a plumber and a builder, a funeral director, a swimming pool engineer, a wine merchant, an interior decorator, an estate agent, an hotelier, a publican and a builder. And all the regular Stevenses who don't have a commercial title.

I suppose I could go through the entire directory, phoning them all and asking about their family history – see if any of them know Daddy. Perhaps not, it would be a huge telephone bill. Next time he phones I'll ask him to give me a lead. Mum says Daddy is not strong on family.

I'd noticed.

Maybe because he was the black sheep of his family, he said, thrown out of the nest. No, that's a mixed metaphor. Sheep don't have nests. He hotfooted it out of town as soon as he could – (another foot metaphor).

Is it fate that Mum brought me here? She could have taken me to any one of a dozen different Cornish towns – Newlyn, Mousehole, Mylor, Penzance, Falmouth. But we came here, to where there are at least a hundred other people called Stevens.

I think I am here to find my lost family, my Daddy's family. He didn't want to be Cornish. He was probably too big for his boots (foot metaphor again).

All I know about them is that Grandad Stevens was a car dealer, and always drove around in smart new cars. Rovers, I think he sold. And Grandma Stevens wore stiff corsets and had pink hair or blue hair and drank her tea with her little finger in the air.

Mum never met them. She says they wouldn't have approved of their son's choice of a much older wife.

She doesn't look her age, Mum, except when she tries to look younger.

Something or someone emptied our dustbin today. Mess everywhere. Mummy was Not Happy. At Peregrine Cottage we would blame a fox, but here in the heart of the town, who knows?

In Essex, where Grandpop and Grandma lived, there was a fox who used to come into their garden each night looking for titbits, (that might be tidbits as titbits sounds rude). I often saw him by the orange street lamp, sauntering across the road and going under their car briefly before doing his usual snacking in their back garden. Grandpop made a habit of leaving food for him. But Grandpop's favourite was the robin. It would follow him around while he was gardening, practically landing on his hoe or spade or whatever. Grandma did most of the gardening but Grandpop was allowed to do the heavy stuff, like digging.

I had a disgusting job to do in her garden – collect caterpillars from the cabbages and drown them in a bucket of water. It didn't occur to me to complain about being hired to torture and murder living creatures.

I wonder how mentally developed a creature has to be before it has a personality. Obviously dogs and cats have personalities, each one a separate identity, like bossy Flo and wimpy Rambo, but what about robins and rats, guinea pigs and toads? If we thought that sheep were interesting characters and have real relationships with each other, would we still kill them for food?

I heard on Radio Four an organic dairy farmer saying that her cows all knew each other and had lasting family relationships. She had witnessed young heifers joyfully greeting their mothers after being separated from them for a year. A joyful cow? What does she do? Jump for joy?

What makes a creature more than just alive? What gives it purpose and contentment, affection for its family?

I do know that certain birds, including swans and geese

and herring gulls, mate for life. But what about insects? If I knew a mosquito had thoughts and feelings and a mother who loved it, would I still want to swat it? What about crabs and prawns? Do they form attachments? Oh dear, I don't want to survive on lentils and bean sprouts and soya beans.

Oh no, I should never have thought about insects dying. Into my cold soup, gazpacho it's called and it's made from chopped tomatoes, has landed a black-fly. He looks like a miniature angel spread-eagled on the red sticky surface – an angel fallen into Hell.

'He'll have tomatoes up his nose,' I say. I can't bear the thought of him drowning slowly so I scoop him out and squash him properly and thoroughly.

'He's got more problems than tomatoes up his nose now,' said Mum, rather callously in my opinion.

When we get home, black-fly and greenfly are everywhere in the garden, all over practically every leaf, and I have frenzy of killing. I don't understand. Why did I feel compassion for one drowning black-fly in my soup and now I am a mad killer with no remorse? I went from being a Buddhist to a maniac mass murderer in less than two hours.

Death: I know, or think I know that death will only be nothingness, but I don't want oblivion yet. I want to smell honeysuckle in the dark, I want to hear my cat greet me with her special purring mew. I want to smell old books. I want everything, clouds, sunshine, I want to see a whale – I've never seen a whale. I even want to hear the terrifying sound of the sea in a storm. I want a boy to kiss me one day. I want to run along a beach again. I want to go to America and Australia. There are so many books I want to read. I want to live.

CHAPTER EIGHT

WE'VE BEEN WATCHING our video of *Casablanca* again. It
never fails to make me cry. Mum too.

Goodbyes: I hate them. At airports, railway stations,
docks – even other people's goodbyes. Even their hellos
make me want to cry: emotion as catching as a virus. When
a child runs and jumps into the open arms of a grandfather;
strangers' tears; other people's happiness, other people's grief
– it gets to me. All those people at the barrier when you go
through customs, you can see the anticipation written in their
eyes, searching for the face of their loved one, the familiar
shape of family. I am moved by their strong feelings. It's as
if it's me they have lost and found again, or I'm a hero come
home from a war. I am affected especially by men's affection,
men hugging their wives or mothers, their children or each
other. That moment when a man hugs another man, perhaps
knowing they won't see each other for a long time, maybe
imagining it's for the last time. Men being affectionate, men
crying. That is so... so... it's wonderful and terrible.

I remember Daddy after Grandpop and Grandma died.
He had been so brave for days, Mum said, phoning friends
to tell them the terrible news. He came to see me in hospital
and suddenly started weeping – silent tears at first. But then
he held my hand tight (he wasn't allowed to hug me as I was
wired up to machines and had tubes coming out of every
orifice) and he gave way to his sadness and really sobbed
for a moment before pulling himself together, controlling
his shaking shoulders and blowing his nose loudly. And they
weren't even his parents. They were Mum's. It was awful to
see him cry. His face didn't dissolve like Mum's does – her
nose goes red and big and spreads all over her cheeks, and

her eyes are puffy for at least twenty-four hours. He looked untouched by his emotion, normal, but with brimming eyes, like a film star who has had glycerine drops to make his eyes glisten. He told me that that's what they do in films. He knows all the tricks of cinematography. That's the art of filming.

I think he should have been a film star instead of a filmmaker. He has that soulful, clapped out look, like Gerard Depardieu or Johnny Halliday or Bruce Willis. I love French films, not only because he does. He once met Jeanne Moreau – his greatest moment, he says.

His favourite movie is *Léon*, directed by Luc Besson. We watched it together in a private cinema in Paris. It was brilliant – lean-back seats as comfortable as armchairs, and there was champagne, well, not for me, obviously, but for Daddy, and he gave me a sip. Even the smell of the place was expensive, as if someone had dropped an entire bottle of lavender oil into the foyer. And the girl – Natalie Portman – when the film was made she was only a little bit older than I am now. Twelve. She's beautiful. And I love her hair, though I think it's rather an expensive looking cut for a girl her age, but maybe all French girls have access to good hairdressers. It's an ace film. Complicated, but with an English soundtrack. Daddy knows all sorts of film people, being in the business.

It's a shame he's lost TLE: The Lovely Eloise. She's very pretty. I wonder why she left. I expect she got bored with being asked if he was her father. Or maybe her career as a model/actress got in the way of a lasting relationship with a man who isn't really going to help her on her way to fame. But that's being sarcastic or...? Oh, I've forgotten the word. Cynical.

I was once accused of being sophisticated by my teacher. I can't remember what I said to her to make her say that. I thought sophisticated was a good thing to be, but no, she said, no, it wasn't. It was very very bad. She made me look it up in the dictionary. I did.

Sophisticated: adulterated; falsified; wordly-wise; devoid or deprived of natural simplicity; complex; very refined or subtle; with qualities produced by special knowledge or skill; (of a person) accustomed to an elegant, cultured way of life; with the most up to date devices.

Maybe Daddy and Mum will get back together. No, I mustn't even think that. She is quite sure she doesn't want to have anything to do with him again. Quite sure. And she's going out with – she has had a date with Alistair. He's nice. Nice is a stupid word, it doesn't convey the feelings I have about him. He's kind. He's quite amusing. He's fairly good looking – if you like horses. He is reassuringly dependable. Not heroic though. Not my idea of a leading man. Maybe when you are as old as Mum, you aren't choosy.

When I was little I invented chip butties – two slices of bread and butter with chips sandwiched between them. I was an unadventurous eater at the time so chip butties were a great step forward for a gourmet-challenged child. I was at last showing an interest. Mum says she had given up trying to make me eat healthy food. It was a losing battle. It was when Mum left me to choose my own lunch-box contents for school that I began to be more adventurous. Dried peaches or apricots, carrots, sunflower seeds, almonds, celery. I was always looking for something no one else had in their lunch box. Oxo Cubes – I had a thing about them for a while. The strong harshness of the flavour. I OD'd I'm afraid. Three of them in one day. Can't stand the smell of them now.

I even liked Spanish wood – that horrible yellow twig that tastes disgusting. I would suck the stick until only the dried fibres remained. I probably needed whatever is in the stuff for a while. I wonder if there is some essential mineral in it? I can't imagine why I would choose to eat it for its flavour.

The drug I had to take regularly when I was a baby helped

regulate my heartbeat. Made from the dried powdered leaves of purple foxglove, it's a steroid which exerts a specific action on the cardiac muscles of animals. A Scottish doctor called William Withering had a patient with a bad heart condition. Withering couldn't help him but the man went to a local gypsy who gave him a medicine made up of all sorts of things including digitalis, and he felt much better. The doctor developed the drug and it was first used medically in 1785. (Alistair told me that. He's Scottish too.)

On my desert island I will eat shellfish – collect mussels and cockles and other bivalves. I am good at that. I could eat bread and butter leaves – if there are blackthorn trees. Grandma showed me them in Essex. I could eat fish – if I could catch them. Maybe I should choose a snorkel and mask as my luxury. I could make a harpoon with a knife from the ship's kitchen tied to a bamboo pole, and a fishing net from coconut husk. Coconuts are amazing trees. You can make the walls, roof and floor of a shelter from the woven dry leaves and a plaited hat from the living leaves. The nut is marvellous food and so is the milk. The husk of the nut is good material for all sorts of things. You can use it as fuel on a fire. And the coconut shell is useful as a cup or bowl. At the base of the stem of the large leaf there's a sort of natural sacking-like fabric that I could make clothes and blankets from. I could eat birds' eggs.

I just had the misfortune to say 'Pardon?'

'Don't say Pardon, say "What"' is Mum's retort.

It was the other way around with Grandma. If I said 'What?' she tut-tutted and said 'Say pardon, dear, "What" is common.'

I just can't win.

It's Saturday: pocket money day. I love mooching around town. It's so easy, only two minutes down the hill. Straight to the library for an hour. There are little children sitting on low seats looking at picture books and trying to read.

'How ya doing, Guss?'

'Brett! G'day!' I hope my Strine impresses him.

'Whatcha reading?'

'It's a book I've read before, but I loved it and want to read it again.'

It's *Blue Lagoon*, by H de Vere Stacpoole – that must be a made up name. He/she must have had a name like Arthur Brown and wanted to sound more interesting or posh. I hope to pick up more hints from the book on how to survive on a desert island.

I have found a book of modern poetry too, an anthology called *Poem for the Day*.

'I've found *The Hitch Hiker's Guide to the Galaxy*. It's beaut,' says Brett.

'What's it about?'

'That's difficult to say. I've only just started it. It's a sort of funny sci-fi. Crazy and cool.'

'Of course! I remember. I've got the towel.'

'Towel?'

He looks at me as if I'm bonkers. This conversation is going wrong.

'Have you been birding lately?' I say desperately, in order to keep him talking.

'Na, too much homework. Half term will be good though – all those exhausted winter arrivals stopping over at Hayle estuary and the Island. Coming for a look?'

'Yes, sure, I expect so.' I must remember to tell Mum. She might drive me.

'When are you starting at school?'

'Dunno.'

Two boys come up to Brett on our way out and he goes off with them. He turns round and winks at me. It makes me feel funny deep inside my tummy. *Is this love?* I ask myself.

I walk away in a dream, and decide to spend some of my money on Pick and Mix sweeties from Woolworths. I like the round flat toffees best and the coloured sugar eggs with chocolate inside. I don't eat the red jellied sweets that look like lips – the E-numbers make me hyper and make my heart race.

There are still a few holiday people around. People with small children who haven't started school yet and old people. There is a group of white-haired Welsh women in Woolworths. They might be clones – all small and round and with tight curls. They are buying everything in sight. Mugs, bath towels, cushions, as if they haven't got shops in Wales. Or as if they are refugees who have been cut off from civilization. Or as if they have been given permission to buy as much as possible in the shortest possible time.

I wander along the harbour, looking over the railing at the high water below. A squall hits the sea and ghosts run under the surface. The gulls are screaming. It's suddenly chilly and I'm glad I wore my denim jacket. The tourist shops are still open, the shell shop and the ice-cream parlour. I look up at a flag flying half-mast above one of the fisherman's lodges and see a black-framed white card stuck inside a glass case. It is a funeral notice. *Arthur Stevens, of St Ives, aged 94, service to be held on Monday next at the Parish Church*. Stevens! He might have been related to me and now he's dead! And I never knew him. It's too late now. Or is it?

CHAPTER NINE

I'M WEARING MY old school navy blue skirt and navy hoodie, and my cricket cap, which is navy blue. It's the closest to funeral clothes that I've got.

'And where are you off to?'

'Library.'

'Didn't you go there Saturday?'

'I'm going again.'

'In school uniform?'

'So?'

'God, why are you so eccentric? Don't be late for lunch.'

'Okay, Bye.'

'Gussie! Take my books back will you?'

'Oh no. They'll be too heavy.'

'There's only two and they aren't heavy.'

'All right.' I have to wait while she searches for her books. She puts them in a carrier bag and gives them to me. Darn it, now I'll have to take them into church with me.

I try to slither past the men in black in the church porch but one touches my arm and asks my name.

'Augusta Stevens,' I blurt, and stay close to a youngish couple with their little girl as if I am part of their family. I have hidden the bag of books in the little garden next to the church, under a seat. I don't think a Tesco bag looks respectful at a funeral.

I slide in to the same pew as the people I followed in and they look at me as if trying to work out who I am, so I smile and they smile back and I pick up the funeral card on the shelf in front. The church is filling up. I've never been in here before. The roof is a concave half-barrel shape, with painted wooden figures of angels or saints at the base of each beam.

The fluted columns and arches are made of carved granite and there's a bible stand shaped like an eagle. The windows are of coloured glass but I can't make out the pictures from this distance. There's a pine coffin on a stand at the front, with brass handles and a wreath on it. Most people are wearing black or dark clothes. I don't look out of place really, though I thought everyone would be wearing hats and I seem to be the only one.

The vicar apologises for the lack of an organist. We stand to sing several hymns: 'All Things Bright and Beautiful'. We used to sing that at school. Then the unaccompanied voices start the words of 'The Lord's My Shepherd'. Some of the men have deep brown voices and they sing in harmony with the lighter voices of the tenors. It's a wonderful sound. I only whisper the words because I start to cry and now I can't stop. It's as if I am saying goodbye to Grandpop and Grandma, not some stranger I might possibly be related to but have never set eyes on. I am crying as if I will never stop, and I haven't brought a tissue with me. My nose streams and my glasses steam up. I'm glad I have my cricket cap to hide under. I wipe my nose and eyes on my sleeve and sniff hard. I can feel the woman in the pew next to me staring, but I keep my head down. She passes me a tissue. I nod.

The vicar drones on, I don't really listen as I am so full of emotion and am desperately trying to control my sobs.

The last hymn is the one with the words 'for those in peril on the sea'. Oh God, that's all I need. Outside I feel exhausted, but relieved somehow of some awful burden. Like a heavy sack of pain. I wonder if the ritual of a service helps people left behind? I missed out on my grandparents' funerals as I was in hospital.

'Are you all right my love?' It's the paper tissue lady.

'Fine, thanks. It was the singing. It got to me. Singing does that sometimes.'

'Are you related?'

'I'm a Stevens,' I say proudly, before sobbing again as I walk away.

On Barnoon Hill I stop several times to catch my breath. Mum's digging a hole in the garden. She hardly looks at me, luckily, as I'm sure my nose is as red as hers when she cries.

'Take my books back?'

Oh, shit, I forgot the books. 'Yeah,' I murmur and go in and collapse on the sofa, where Charlie immediately comes to console me. Thank God for cats.

It occurs to me that I have become a curser, a bad mouth, a swearer, a blasphemer. In my head mostly, but I didn't used to be. It must be because I am growing up. Or maybe because I am lying and cheating I am becoming decadent. No longer innocent. If Grandma and Grandpop were still alive they would be horrified. Oh dear. Am I a lost soul? Am I utterly sophisticated and condemned to a life of deceit?

CHAPTER TEN

IN THE BLUE LAGOON there's all sorts of handy hints on survival on a tropical island.

Breadfruit trees are common and the fruit, which looks rather like a lumpy green lemon, can be barbecued or baked and eaten when the skin bursts. The important thing is to have the means of making fire. In those days they had something called a tinder-box. I think it contained flint and steel for producing a spark to set light to dry twigs or grass.

Grandma used to keep a box of Swan Vestas in the bathroom where their loo was. She swore by them. After you have had a poo you light one or two matches and they make bad smells disappear. Mum does the same thing. It's a trick she's inherited. It really works. It's the sulphur I think. It sort of eats odours. Perhaps if I always have a box in my pocket, the chances are they'd survive a shipwreck with me. I'd only have to light one fire and keep it burning forever, and I wouldn't need any more matches. I like the design on the box: white swan on green lake floating to red sky.

I go back for the bag of books in the garden but it rained in the night and they are sodden and curled at the corners. I shove them into a waste bin and leave, trying not to catch the eye of the tramp in the shelter. He sells the *Big Issue* in Fore Street sometimes, but now he's given in to the demon drink, I think. His eyes are pink and piggie. I wonder if he looked at the books and rejected them. Perhaps he's not interested in *Small Garden Design* and *Building a Wildlife Pond*. He could have used them to wipe his bottom though, like Grandma said they used to do. She would cut up sheets of newspaper into squares and thread them onto string to hang in the lavatory. They had an Elsan lavatory that Grandpop emptied once a week. He called it 'Burying the dead'. Maybe book paper is too thick and shiny to be suitable for bum wiping.

I never know whether to give money to beggars. Not that there are any here. But in London there are loads. I feel so sorry for them, especially the young ones. Dad always gives them money, but Mum doesn't believe in it.

I remember a girl in Southend Green, next to Hampstead Heath. She was sitting on a blanket in the doorway of a closed shop. Mum goes into the café next door and buys her a cheese and tomato sandwich and a cup of soup and tells her to go to the nearest shelter for the night. She must be only about fifteen. What must she have gone through to leave home and live on the street? Is she on drugs? Is she a prostitute? Has someone in her family been really cruel to her, abused her? I never find out of course. I'm too scared to ask and she's gone next time I go past. I ask Mum why she didn't just bring her home with us.

'Gussie,' she said, 'Don't you think we have More than Enough Problems at the Moment without Looking for More?'

She's right of course, but I feel very frustrated not being able to do anything for homeless people. Mum says it's a government issue. If everyone votes for whoever they believe in, the country might stand a chance of being run properly and maybe there would be no homeless people on the streets. She does buy the *Big Issue* though.

Dad isn't really homeless as he rents a flat in London, but I am Dadless and Mum is husbandless.

CHAPTER ELEVEN

I KNOW WHY I chose the attic over the other more accessible rooms for my bedroom.

It's because attics and towers are where heroes and heroines are incarcerated in fairy tales. Rapunzel hung her long hair out of the tower window so her lover could climb up to her. The little princes didn't do very well in their tower, did they? And *Childe Roland to the Dark Tower came*. In *Jane Eyre* there's a mad woman shut in the attic. A poor servant girl sleeps in a garret in the Hans Andersen fairy tale 'The Bottle Neck'. I wonder if *A Room of One's Own* is an attic? It probably is. And of course, poor Anne Frank had to hide from the Nazis in an Amsterdam attic.

My room is a warm nest in the roof, close to the sky, above all the ordinary life of the town. It's especially wonderful with the gulls to keep me company. They are totally oblivious of humans except when we seem to threaten their young: open a window near the nest, open a curtain, that sort of thing.

Our juvenile is a pain in the bum. He's still wheezing and whingeing all day long, lowering his gawky head between his speckled shoulders and having a good grizzle. I'm surprised his mother hasn't pushed him over the edge of the roof and *made* him fly. Perhaps he's flight-featherly challenged or frightened of heights. Perhaps I should be sorry for him but I have more sympathy for his long-suffering parents. Only a parent could love an adolescent herring gull.

After my bath I search my armpits and crotch for signs of hair but no luck yet. I'm pubicly challenged.

I apply cream lavishly to my itchy scar but it doesn't help for more than a minute or two. If I do ever have a boyfriend

I won't want him to see my scar. It's hideous: red and lumpy. Mum says it is Of No Importance. Anyway, if I have a heart-lung transplant, I will be opened up again like a can of beans, or rather, like a box of cornflakes, so there's not much point in worrying about this particular bodily flaw. My friend Summer worries about her looks all the time, even though she's very pretty. She wants to be taller, thinner, blonder.

I would just like to be pinker.

I hang the *Hitch Hiker's Guide to the Galaxy* bath towel out of the window to dry.

Daddy was a great fan of the radio serial years ago and still quotes stuff from it like 'Don't panic' – and he bought Mummy this towel years ago, before I was born, but now it's mine. It's a faded red-brown on one side and white on the other, has frayed ends and a message woven into it. When I'm in the bath and can't read a book I try to read the words on the towel. That's not easy without glasses, but as I practically know it off by heart I guess some of the words.

It goes something like this.

The Hitch Hiker's Guide has lots to say about towels. A towel is just about the most useful thing you can take with you, because you can dry yourself, use it as a weapon when it's wet, wrap yourself in it to keep warm, and use it as a sail. It's also of psychological value as any strag (non hitch-hiker) would think that anyone who can keep his towel with him through all the perils of galaxy travel is a man to be reckoned with. 24/25.

I'm not sure what 24/25 means. It might be the date or it might be that our towel is number 24 out of 25 that were produced, like photographers write on their limited edition prints. That would make it very rare and valuable one day, if it was in perfect condition, which it certainly isn't. But it would be an excellent thing to have with me on my desert island.

I am going to take more photographs. I've decided. I have taken a few of the cats, but they move too much and I can't keep refocusing with my glasses on or off.

There's still unexposed pictures on my film. I hope the washing line photos look okay.

The fisherman's lodges are little shacks on the harbour wall. A flag flies at half-mast. Shamrock Lodge is on its own at the top of a slipway next to the Sloop Inn. On the wooden walls there are faded photographs of lovely old fishing boats with brown sails. The harbour was once a forest of masts. There's a metal stove, unlit of course, because it's still summer, just about; benches around the walls and long tables. In here you feel like you are in another time, shut away from the noise of tourists.

I feel shy of taking pictures of the men playing dominoes, but they are very relaxed about me being here. When I knocked at the door and asked if I could take some pictures they said they didn't mind.

'School project, is it?' a small thin man asks.

'Something like that.'

'Saw you in parish church last week, didn't us, my cheel'? Arthur Stevens' funeral?'

'I'm Gussie Stevens.'

'You'm one of we, my girl.'

One of we? One of us. I feel proud. I feel like an impostor.

'I'm Jackson Stevens' daughter. He lives in London but my mother and I live here now.'

'Up London eh?'

'He's a filmmaker.' (He is, sort of.)

'Following in his footsteps are you?'

'Following in his footsteps? Oh, I suppose I am.' Another foot metaphor!

A herring gull stomps around on the roof, screeching

angrily. The four men go back to their dominoes.

I take off my glasses and focus on the men's faces. They are tanned and lined like Grandpop's was by life, sorrow and laughter; their pale eyes used to looking at the far horizon. I suddenly see they are so much more beautiful than young faces, which are blank empty pages.

They wear flat caps, except one who wears a battered sea captain's cap. They ignore me, intent on the game, slapping down the little bricks with a loud crack on the wooden table. I always thought dominoes was a pointless game needing little or no skill, but the men are concentrated, passionate. There must be more to it than I thought.

Alistair says cricket is like that. It gets more interesting the more you study it. He's taking Mum and me to a game on Saturday. Do I really want to go and watch a load of men try to hit a bunch of sticks with a ball? Or another man try to hit the ball with a stick?

I remove one film from the camera and replace it with another. I include the thick shaft of light striping the dark wall and floor, the pictures, the old radio on a shelf. They are keeping a part of their old life alive in this little hut. I take a picture of a motto in Cornish on the wall – *Meor ras ma Dew*. 'Great thanks to God.'

So Porthmeor means great beach, I suppose.

'Have you been to Shore an' Rose?'

'What's shorn rose?'

'The other two lodges, my flower, other side of slip.'

'Will it be all right for me to go there?'

'Aye, they won't mind. We're used to being looked at. We'm a dying breed.'

'Oh, no,' I'm embarrassed and don't know what to say. Do I look like I'm studying them as if they are pigmies or aboriginals?

'Tell 'em you're a Stevens. 'Es, one o' we.'

I thank them, put on my glasses, pick up the empty film cassette and leave.

There are still plenty of holiday people around, mostly the 'tea and pee brigade' or Saga louts, Mum calls them, coach parties of elderly people hugging the narrow pavements and using walking sticks like weapons. They seem to be having a lovely time. They have North Country and Birmingham accents, so I expect they aren't used to white sand and blue sea.

It makes me smile when a man with a Chelsea Football T-shirt has his carton of chips stolen from his hands by a clever gull. He turns his head for a moment and suddenly his chips are gone. He looks so surprised. They're genius scavengers.

There are letters to the local paper about the 'gull problem' nearly every week, but I think the answer lies not in a gull cull, but in people not eating pasties and chips in the streets. I'm on the gulls' side in this. Give me gulls over people eating smelly food in the street any time. Perhaps the local council or whoever makes decisions should stop allowing fast food outlets in the town. But I suppose they need the money.

I give the other fishermen's lodges a miss, as I'm tired. It takes it out of me, walking and doing things. I'm spending today in bed, veging out. Mum has taken my film to be developed in Penzance.

She has made a little pond in our garden. She's planted a miniature bamboo next to it and we have put in the proper oxygenating weeds. Can't wait for Mr Toad to discover it and entice a mate to lay eggs there next spring. I like watching tadpoles.

I hope we get newts. Mum said when she was little she bought a newt from a girl over the road who had a huge pond, to put in Grandma's tiny pond that was part of a rockery, and the newt disappeared, so she bought another one from the same girl. One day she saw her newt crossing the road, making for his old pond. She was really mad. She'd spent her pocket money on the same newt. When she was ten she was walking in a marshy field near a pond with two friends and one of them picked up a creature from the grass. It's a lizard, she said. Mum said, 'No it isn't, it's a newt,' and to prove it she took it and threw it into the water, where they watched it drown. Her friends didn't speak to her for ages, and she has Never Forgiven Herself. She hasn't had much luck with newts. Perhaps this time it will be different.

I have a terrarium in my room. It's actually a fish tank with no water. Instead it has earth, stones and little plants from the hedge. I'm going to catch a lizard and keep it for a while to study it. I've seen a few on the hedge in front of the house and I am keeping watch for one right now. Charlie's sitting patiently next to me, hoping I'm after some tasty four-legged furry creature for her tea. Well, no, I don't think you'd like lizard sandwich, Charlie.

CHAPTER TWELVE

MUM'S GOT A renewal reminder from the library. Luckily, I get to the post before she does and put the letter in my pocket.

To play for time I go to the library and renew the books. I can hardly tell Mum I left them in the Memorial Gardens while I attended the funeral of someone I didn't know.

But what can I tell her? Or shall I just tell the library the books are lost and pay for them?

It's like the horse story when I was at Sunday School. I told my Sunday School teacher I had a horse when I didn't, and the lie followed me like a malevolent spirit until I was found out. I haven't told a lie since, until I threw away the books. I'm in deep shit.

Mum has always said that telling lies is a complete no-no. It's because of Daddy, of course. She said she can't ever trust him again, since his infidelity with TLE.

Why did I lie about the books? Guilt, self-preservation, denial. She would be shocked that I went to a complete stranger's funeral. Mum doesn't really want me to contact Daddy's family. She acts as if she's angry with them as well as Daddy. But it's my family too. My family! I'm angry with her. It's her fault I have to lie to her. Why can't I tell her that? She doesn't realise she's forcing me into a life of deception. I'll spend sleepless nights of scheming and skulduggery. I'll be cunning and shifty, sneaky and furtive, so much more interesting than being honest and open, except I don't think I can keep it up. It's too wearing. Perhaps the library people will give up. Perhaps I could go and tell them she has left the country and I think she took the books with her because she needs *Small Garden Design* and *Building a Wildlife Pond* in Australia. Perhaps not. Anyway, it's hardly first-degree murder is it, lying? Or maybe it is the first step towards hell and damnation.

My lizard is boring. He stands on a twig and stares at nothing. There's plenty of garden stuff in there with him, like leaves and earth and pebbles, but he doesn't seem interested in exploring. Perhaps he's depressed, being imprisoned and observed. I find a grasshopper for him to eat. It takes ages. I thought it would be easy, but it isn't. I feel terrible choosing a creature to be sacrificed. I have all this power to destroy.

Once when I was visiting Grandma and Grandpop I was on the stone jetty near where they lived, watching boys fishing for crabs, and I was horrified when the boys jumped on the crabs, crushed them with their shoes and threw them back. I had thought they were going to take them off the mussel bait and put them back in the water. I shouted at them and when they laughed at me I pushed one of the boys in. It wasn't deep but it was cold and he was suitably humiliated. His friend couldn't stop laughing so I pushed him in too. I have a quick temper, Grandma says – said. I inherited it from my mother.

My lizard has grabbed the grasshopper by its back legs and has been hanging on to it for ages, simply sucking it. Why doesn't it swallow it? I have been watching it for half an hour and the lizard hasn't moved. It's as if it is paralysed. The doomed grasshopper occasionally jerks in a feeble attempt to escape the jaws of the dragon, but the lizard, grim-mouthed, keeps hold. I don't like the lack of expression in its eyes. I used to be fond of lizards, I'm not so sure now. I can't watch any more, it's horrible. The grasshopper will die from starvation and terror before it gets eaten. What do grasshoppers eat, anyway? I'll release the lizard tomorrow.

Maybe insects should be my line of study, or spiders. I don't mind them. Mum does. She cringes when one gets in the bath and I have to rescue it for her. There are little black jumping spiders in the grass. They leap about to escape me when I try to catch them. I like the long-legged garden spiders best. They walk slowly as if balancing on stilts, blown off balance by the slightest breeze. Their legs are like fine human hair.

We don't have a spider book. I miss all the old books on wildlife there were at Peregrine Cottage. I think I'll start spending pocket money on second-hand books. There's always a good selection at the car boot sales and there's a big second-hand bookshop in town.

I find a good spider book – *The Spiders and Allied Orders of the British Isles* by Theodore H Savory.

Pholcidae – very long-legged spider – lives in southeast counties of England, but we are in the far southwest, so maybe this isn't my long-legged spider. I'm pretty sure it isn't because ours has a round body and this has a long body. Bet there aren't any books on Cornish spiders. I've found it. It's *Leiobnum rotundum*. 'Only the male's body is round. It is rusty brown with no obvious markings apart from the black eye-turret. The female's body is oval and paler with a dark, more or less rectangular saddle. Both sexes have long, hair-like black legs.'

I have liberated the lizard with SED – Sadistic Eating Disorder. Now I have an empty terrarium. I remember when I was little we had a silk worm farm at school. I wonder where we got the leaves for it? Silk worms only eat mulberry leaves. And I had an ant farm once in a large jam jar, and a worm farm in between two sheets of glass that Grandpop made for me.

Our little pond is already swarming with life, mosquito larvae mostly, *Culex pipiens* probably as they are the most common. They wriggle under water, jerkily, but when I get close to the pond they dive backwards together and disappear, like formation swimmers in a Busby Berkeley movie. We bought two water snails, *Limniaea stagnalis* I think they are, but they seem to have mated and produced lots of babies. Jumping Jiminy Cricket, that was quick work. There's loads of Daphnia, or water fleas.

I have an *Observer's Book of Pond Life*. There are some wonderful water bugs I've never heard of: Water Cricket, Water Measurer, Long Water Scorpion and Pond Skater. The only one I have heard of is the Water Boatman.

Bugs possess a sucking beak called a rostrum with which most of them pierce their prey and suck out their juices. Yuk, even life in our little pond is fraught with danger.

Then there are the water beetles: Mud Dweller, Great Silver Beetle, Screech Beetle, Great Diving Beetle, and there's even a Whirligig Beetle. Fly and moth larvae and pupae lurk in the vegetation near the surface. Water mites and water spiders live in ponds too. It's going to be crowded. With luck we'll have Damsel Flies and Dragon Flies.

Perhaps we should turn the whole garden into a pond with little bridges for the cats to walk over.

Mr Toad hunkers in his John Innes compost bag. I wonder if he thinks he is John Innes, with his name on the door of his home, like Winnie the Pooh's friend, Piglet, who lived in a house with a notice that said TRESPASSERS W. Piglet said it had been in his family for generations and his Grandfather's name was William and that is what the w stood for.

CHAPTER THIRTEEN

I AM FEELING rather miserable today. Daddy phoned. He's off to some film festival in France. I don't know why I did it, maybe to escape from the wrath of Mum and the library authorities, but I suddenly blurted out 'Can I come too?' He says he can't be looking after me while he's in conference with directors and producers etc. Sure. Yeah, I understand. I'll be in the way. He'll be looking for a replacement for The Lovely Eloise. Some new young starlet with fake tits and legs up to her armpits. What if my donor heart and lungs are suddenly available and we have to go to London straight away? He won't be there. Where will Mummy stay? He won't be at my bedside. I don't want him to leave the country. I don't want them to be divorced. *I need a family.*

I spend the day in my attic, my turret room, my garret, my lofty tower, the cats surrounding me, trying to comfort me. Rain hammers on the roof, and the wind is howling in sympathy with my emotions. I am a victim, a hard-done-by heroine with the world against me. No one understands me except Charlie, who curls up on my tummy and gazes at me sorrowfully with her viridian eyes.

'Gussie! Gussie! There's someone for you.'

I ignore Mum. It's probably the library police. I've been shopped by the tramp, the only witness of my crime and delinquency. (I found that word in our *Chambers*. It means *failure or omission of duty*.)

'Gussie!'

'What?'

'It's Brett for you.'

Oh brill! Brett's come to see me. I dry my tears, brush my hair and clean my glasses. Oh shit, I should never look in a mirror. I am always dismayed. What do I imagine I look like? Not this puny, pale-mauve shrimp with a red nose, that's for sure.

He comes up and has to bend down to miss the beams on the ceiling, he's so tall.

'How's it goin?'

I *lurv* his accent and he doesn't seem to notice my nose, or he's too polite to comment.

He says hello to the cats and scratches Charlie behind her ears. He's good with animals. He looks out the window and admires the view and we watch the young gull for a while. He says he and his dad have a herring gull's nest on their roof too. Most people in St Ives are lucky enough to have gulls living close to them. Brett's gull comes right into their house and walks around looking for titbits. Since I was ill in the summer, he and his dad have hand-raised a young raven they found under a bush. Brett's mum gets very cross because Buddy the raven tears off wallpaper and picks up newspaper pages and tears them up. He follows Brett on his bicycle down the road, flying close to his head all the time even when a car goes by.

'I'd love to meet Buddy.'

'You will,' he says, and then, 'You aren't really reading *Roget's Thesaurus* for fun, are you?'

'Yeah, it's interesting. Listen: "Deceitful – false; fraudulent, sharp, guileful, insidious, slippery as an eel, shifty, tricky, cute, finagling, chiselling, underhand, underhanded, furtive, surreptitious, indirect, collusive, covinous, falsehearted." Oh dear, falsehearted – that's what I will be when I have my transplant.'

He laughs loudly.

'Gussie, you are so weird.' He knocks off my England cricket cap with a brush of his hand and tousles my hair. No one's ever done that, apart from Grandpop.

'The rain's stopped, Guss, let's go birding.'

He has his binoculars around his neck.

'Okay' I say, nonchalantly. 'Cool. Rippa.' I grab my bins, retrieve my cap and we go downstairs to tell Mum we're off to the Island.

'Are you sure you want to go? You look pale. Take your parka. Have you got your bleep?'

'Mum, I'm not stupid.'

Brett manages to walk slowly enough so I don't get left behind. I'm not very good at talking as I walk, not enough breath for both activities, but he doesn't seem to notice. He rambles on about what he's been doing this term. I wish I was at school too.

We walk around the harbour. Sparrows and starlings peck at the ground hopefully. The Island is just around the corner from the harbour, next to Porthgwidden Beach. It's a peninsula really, not an island at all, but that's what it's called. In the old days locals used to spread their sheets out on the grass slopes to dry in the sun.

It's windy on the Island, but I don't mind. My cap is firmly on my head and I am wrapped up well. I've got my ex-army parka that we bought at Laurence Corner. Quilted and warm. Mum took up the sleeves for me. I'm also wearing camouflage fatigue trousers with lots of pockets. It's a good idea to wear natural colours when bird-watching. That way you merge into the background. We shelter by a large rock covered in green and yellow lichens, out of the wind and with a good view of the sea and sky out towards the northwest, under the coastguard lookout. The crashing of the waves is muffled here. There's a smell of salt and grass. Huge orange and dark grey cumulus clouds lollop heavily across the silver sky. It's like autumn already.

There have been sunfish spotted from here in hot weather. I've never seen a sunfish.

We watch the cormorants flying low over the waves; shearwaters and oystercatchers, each bird so beautiful in its individual flight pattern and behaviour. A flock of starlings swirling like mist over the fields and snaking the hedges; a v of airborne geese yapping like dogs; swans gliding effortlessly on a river, or in flight, the wind whistling through their great white wings.

We love birds in spite of the fact that some eat each other's babies; some kill better singers (robins) and are often barbaric in their behaviour, except to their own mates and young. I think it is because they are beautiful that we overlook their actions. Beauty can do anything and we still adore it. Our eyes, our hearts and souls need beauty.

Brett says he's going to the Hayle estuary next week in case some of the winter birds are arriving. They stop over here after flying across the Atlantic Ocean, and they rest up on this, the first bit of land they find, to gather strength and build up their body weight. He says I can go with him and his dad if I want. You bet I want.

From our sheltered spot we see various gulls: skua, fulmar, Great Black-backed gull, gannet, herring gull of course, black headed gull, tern, cormorant, oyster catcher, shag, and some little diving ducks in a flotilla.

'Gussie, you're blue.'

'I'm always blue.'

'No, you're darker blue than usual; your lips are purple. You look bushed. We better get you home.'

'Okay, I am a bit cold.' I'm so glad it's his idea, not mine. I'm bloody freezing.

We set off, Brett carrying my binoculars. We stop at the seat on the hill while I squat to catch my breath, pretending to do up my shoes.

'I don't suppose you could come to the Scillies in October, could you? A birding weekend.'

'I don't know.' Mum would never let me go on my own. Oh, I really want to go. We've never been to the Scillies.

'How are you getting there?'

'Helicopter to St Mary's, then a boat. An organised trip. Your Ma's friend is going.'

'Alistair?'

'Yeah, I reckon. The doctor?'

'Yes, our GP. He's keen on my mum.'

'Yeah? Well, she's cool.'

A cunning plan has occurred to me. Oh dear, I really am becoming scheming and wily.

CHAPTER FOURTEEN

WE ARE IN a field next to the secondary school.

In the next field are three horses: a tall skewbald, much bigger than the others, a little fat Shetland pony and a cream palomino. The Shetland pony is tearing around the field, his mane and tail horizontal, and the other horses are following him, joining in the fun. When he stops they stop. They are all speaking to each other; neighing and snorting like Wild West ponies. They are having such a good time.

Eleven men in cream trousers and white shirts and cream woolly jumpers with stripes around the v-neck are standing around while two batsmen stand at either end of the pitch. There are two umpires wearing what look like white laboratory coats. There's a smell of grass and bonfires and the sea. Gulls chuckle overhead. We are two of about ten people watching – most of them are in the batting side. Alistair is one of the batsmen. He goes to hit the ball and misses. Mum groans. He misses again. Oh dear. The bowler bowls again and Alistair whacks the ball hard and a fielder tries to stop it but it goes to the boundary and it's a four. We applaud loudly.

I think of Grandpop and Grandma playing cricket together and I feel sad and happy at the same time. Mum isn't the least bit sporty, though she did do a yoga class once but her back went so she didn't go again. Alistair looks very dashing in his cricket whites.

Mum is smart and pretty in navy linen baggy trousers, sleeveless white top and white linen hat. She's got war-paint on too, glossy shiny lip stuff and mascara. I prefer her with no make-up.

I wear my England cricket cap of course. I feel it's really

mine now, after wearing it every day for several weeks. It is getting nicely battered and comfortable.

A very angry sounding gull is chasing a buzzard, who lazily lifts a wing when the gull gets close enough to peck at it and soars higher and higher, effortlessly. The gull is satisfied and goes home. Two crows squabble in a tall pine between the school and the field. There's a far view of the bay and you can see as far as Carn Brea and right along the coast to Newquay.

The other batsmen waiting for their turn are chattering away all the time. When each one gets given 'out' by the umpire, he comes back very cross and blames the bat, the wind, and/or the other batsman – and especially the blind umpire.

Suddenly the wind drops to nothing and the sun burns us. Swallows swoop low over the grass, flashing purple and blue wings. There's a strange thick band of sea mist hovering over the horses' field. It's coming towards us, a white fog, like a low spiralling cloud, and suddenly the sun has gone and we are shivering. A phantom juvenile herring gull whistles. The horses have disappeared.

We go inside the cricket pavilion, where it's much warmer, and sit huddled together, looking out through the doorway. It's hilarious: the players are hidden in mist. The occasional head appears, moving fast, or an arm and hand thrown up into the air. It's a match between invisible men. A clunk, a shout, and the red ball runs out of the fog and over the boundary, hit by a ghost Alistair I think.

'Four,' shouts one of the spectators and throws the ball back into the whiteness.

Inside the hut a woman is busy setting sandwiches and cakes on plates. A little girl, about six years old, is helping her. Oh strewth, it's the woman who was in the same pew as me at the funeral. I hide under my cap and put up the collar of my parka. I don't think she's noticed me. That's the trouble with a small town. You keep bumping into the same people.

The local team is out, which means they've all been bowled or caught or run out, or were called out LBW – leg before wicket – and they all come inside. Time for tea. The little girl runs to her daddy, who is one of the local team, and he lifts her up and kisses her.

The sea-mist has gone as quickly as it appeared so we go outside again, thank goodness. Alistair gets his plate of sandwiches and cakes and brings them out for us to share. He gets Mum and me cups of tea. He's quite pleased with himself as he scored 55 runs. He says he should have got more: it's a flat wicket, whatever that means.

The team is a great mix of people: there's the vicar, a policeman, a convicted burglar (just out of prison, Alistair says, and when he isn't being a burglar he's usually a night club bouncer) a schoolboy, a barman, an undertaker, a cabinet maker, a teacher, a double-glazing fitter, a window cleaner, and a doctor, Alistair. He plays for a cricket team of doctors in Cornwall too, and he says they are going to play on the Scillies soon. They'll stay on St Mary's, and hire a boat to play on St Agnes and Tresco over a long weekend.

This is my cue. If I miss it now, I'll never get another chance.

'Mum, can we go too? I've always wanted to go to the Scillies. Oh, Mum, please.'

'Yes, what a good idea, Gussie,' says Alistair, 'I could try and get you into my hotel.'

'Well, I don't know. How much will it cost?' Mum is looking for problems.

It's time for the other team to bat and Alistair has to field so we don't get a chance to come to any decisions.

We watch for a little, while the men's green shadows get longer and longer in the low sun. The horses are standing quietly, dozing on their hooves.

Mum drives me home and we pick up Indian take-away. Chicken chilli masala, pashwari nan, tarka dhall, rice and pappadoms. Yum.

Charlie takes up a ringside seat so I can feed her spicy chicken. Flo only likes the pappadoms.

We sit on the floor on cushions and eat from the low table, as we're watching a movie, *Local Hero*. I've seen it three times. There's a baby in a buggy that gets pushed around by various men throughout the story. I love the bit when the American asks who the baby's father is, and the men look shifty and no one answers. It's a car-free little village in Scotland, and every time the American goes onto the street he nearly gets run down by a moped. Also, the music is great. It reminds me of going to see movies with Daddy in London.

Oh, why did he have to leave? Mum is much better looking than any of those anorexics he runs after. She might be crotchety sometimes, but she's a good cook and hasn't let herself go to pot just because she's old.

Charlie hangs around until I give her some chicken. She prefers spicy meat to ordinary cat food and if ever she smells coriander she's sniffing the air and looking at me beseechingly. I clear away the dirty dishes and load the dishwasher in an attempt to keep Mum sweet.

'Mum, can we go to the Scillies, ple-ease.'

'I'll think about it, darling.'

Alistair rings the next day and says there's no accommodation left in St Mary's. It's always difficult getting a room there, apparently, and you have to book up weeks in advance.

'Brett is birdwatching in the Scillies in October, could we go then?'

'Birdwatching? I don't particularly like birdwatching. Anyway, there's nothing for me to do in the Scillies.'

'Mum, you are so selfish. I like birdwatching. I could go on my own. You don't have to come.'

'On your own?'

'With Brett and his mum and dad.'

'But we don't know them. No, definitely not. Maybe another time, darling.'

'What other time? I might not have another time,' I shout.

'Gussie, that's emotional blackmail. I'm ashamed of you.'

'Anyway, Alistair is going.' I hurl that titbit at her, slam the door, climb up to my room, wishing I could run, and have a good cry. I haven't even got the consolation of cats as I shut them in the sitting room.

I hate feeling in the wrong or wronged. Somehow, everything has gone badly lately: not being able to start at the school, ruining the library books, crying at the funeral, not getting anywhere with the search for my Cornish family, and now this.

I really want to go to the Scillies.

I can't go anywhere or do anything any more. I feel all knotted up and twisted inside my head and stomach.

CHAPTER FIFTEEN

I DON'T BELIEVE it. Mum is dressed in shorts and T-shirt and trainers and she's going for a run with Alistair. She still has the full make-up, her hair is tied back and she has sweatbands on her wrists and forehead.

'You aiming on perspiring, Mum?'

'I might.' She takes a long look at herself in the full-length mirror.

'Is my bum saggy?'

'Yes it is. You should be in purdah.'

'Thanks, Gussie darling. See you later.'

I'm sitting in the front garden in the sunshine under the sun-brolly, reading. The washing line next door is full of striped sheets flapping in the wind, though I didn't see who put them there.

Half an hour later Alistair brings Mum home. She's done something to her back. They were running along Porthmeor Beach and she made the mistake of twisting her head round to enjoy the view of the sea and 'Something Went.' That'll teach her to try and act younger than her age.

She lies on the sofa and he gets her a painkiller and a whisky. He says scotch is a good analgesic, or was it anaesthetic? Why doesn't he rub it on her back then?

'Gussie, can you keep an eye on her tonight? I think she may have damaged a disc.'

Oh great. *I'm* going to have to look after *her* now. I fill up a hot water bottle and put it on her back and get a blanket to cover her.

'Mum, do you know you've got hairy toes?' Cripes, I hope I don't get hairy toes.

'Oh shut up Gussie, just shut up.'

She starts to cry. She looks awful. I fill up her whisky glass.

'Oh that's Far Too Much, darling,' she says, but drinks it anyway.

CHAPTER SIXTEEN

MUM HAS MADE a friend: the physiotherapist who is sorting out her back. We go to visit her at her house in Horsetown – spelt Halsetown – a mile or so outside St Ives. It's so quiet and peaceful here among the granite outcrops, hardly any topsoil on the hills, just gorse and heather and furze, the eerie cry of buzzards wheeling above us, buttercups and daisies in the little fields, an invisible skylark singing.

There's a little boy; he's eight, called Gabriel. There's also Phaedra, sixteen, and Troy, fifteen, who aren't there today as they are surfing. Gabriel shows me his floppy-eared rabbits, two of them, lolloping around on the grass, and three stand-up straight ducks, mother, father and daughter, who are worrying the grass with their beaks. One of them is lame but is still a good layer, he says. A large pond is fed by a little stream. The ducks don't ever go in the pond; they prefer the grass. Gabriel says there are frogs and toads and newts, but we don't see any. There's a golden cockerel with a very fine tail and smart red comb, two brown hens and six chicks. The mother hen is in protective custody in a little triangular hut and pen with her babies. One is black and the others are yellow. The black one spends most of its time on its mother's back. Gabriel saves the best until last. We go upstairs and he opens the airing cupboard door and there on the bottom shelf on a layer of blankets and towels is their tabby cat, Treasure, with four kittens, three tabby and one black. They are three weeks old. The kittens tumble over each other and wobble on shaky legs. Treasure, whose original name was Tricia, but they changed it, looks very proud of herself. She is less than a year old, and this is her first litter, but she is a good mother, very attentive to her babies. There's a tomcat too, Spider, who is tabby and white, not the father, as he's been neutered, but he nevertheless brings Treasure mice every day.

Gabriel, having done his tour guide duty by me, races off and the next time I see him he is up a tree, wielding a full-sized saw and a hammer. He has made a whole system of platforms and roofs in the oak tree. His dad makes staircases and furniture and built their entire house. There's a sign – James Darling and Son, Cabinet Makers – by the gate. There's a painting of a staircase on the sign. Gabriel has obviously inherited a talent for building things.

His mum, whose name is Claire, says Gabriel spends most of his time up the tree, only coming down to go to school or sleep or eat, though sometimes he takes his tea up there. He has fixed a rope and pulley to get himself up into the branches. There's also a Tarzan rope for swinging on.

I wander around the garden, following the ducks and rabbits. There's a herb garden with bronze fennel and mint, clumps of thyme and basil and the tallest sunflowers, and huge bushes of lavender; a vegetable plot with potatoes and bean-poles, and a huge sweet-smelling poly-tunnel for salad vegetables, aubergines, tomatoes, pak choi and other exotic vegetables I don't recognise. One part of the garden has been left wild, like a meadow, with all sorts of wild flowers – poppies, cornflowers, hemp agrimony and tall feathery grasses. Butterflies and bees love this place. So would I if I was a butterfly.

My favourite thing in the garden is a little hut tucked behind the house, a cabin, with a rounded roof made of corrugated metal, a little like a gypsy caravan. There's a deck all round it with potted scarlet pelargoniums and marigolds, and a little garden of its own with white and grey pebbles in patterns around the plants.

I am desperate to look inside. I can't see Mum or Claire to ask permission, but I make an executive decision, climb the wooden steps and peep through the red checked curtains of the window. There's no one in. It looks very tidy: a sofa, a single divan bed with a red-checked blanket on it and a low table at one end by the stove, the kitchen and table at the other end and a bead curtain doorway to the bathroom, I suppose. There's a bookshelf and a framed old photograph, a black and white portrait of a girl, slender, frizzy-haired, in a white muslin frock. She holds a posy of flowers. It could be a wedding photo.

A stream runs alongside the cabin, with a little wooden bridge over it where a large fluffy tabby sits watching me watching her. 'Hello,' I say to her, but she turns her head away and gazes haughtily into the stream, where tiny brown trout flash in the sun.

Beyond the stream are huge Scots pines with broken off lower branches, and young crows making a horrible din as if they are strangling each other. Hidden cows moo and breathe heavily in the next field. There's a poem about the cow I read the other day – something about one end milk the other moo.

We eat tea under an apple tree, with a blanket spread on the grass. There's fresh bread baked by Gabriel's dad, who appears briefly and makes himself a sandwich.

'Saw you with Alistair, didn't I, at cricket, Saturday?'

'Oh yes,' says Mum, 'I thought I recognised you, you were batting with him, weren't you?'

'He's a proper batsman, not like me. He can hit it.'

We stuff ourselves with crabmeat, ham, cheese and salad. Then summer pudding with cream. The floppy-eared rabbits, ducks and chickens go ambling by in their own little worlds, intent on searching for food. Wasps try their luck but no one gets stung.

I think of Grandma and her wasp trap: a jammy jam-jar half full of water. The unsuspecting wasp crawls into the pot after the sweetness and stickiness and drowns. She was a stealthy killer, my Grandma. She had a running battle with caterpillars and spiders. No cobwebs allowed in her house.

I'm always arguing with Mum about cobwebs. She seems to think they shouldn't be in the corners of rooms or wrapped around the lampshades or books, but what about the poor little spiders that depend on food that gets caught in their traps: bluebottles and fruit flies, wasps and other flying insects? She hates those, so she should encourage spiders. I expect she's inherited her arachnophobia from her mother. I think she enjoys wielding the very beautiful feather duster I gave her once for a birthday. It is made of ostrich feathers. I should never have given it to her. Perhaps I could hide it. I wonder what those very thin spiders you find in kitchen drawers live on? And old shoe boxes? What do they find to survive on in enclosed spaces? Mites or something, I suppose.

Treasure joins us and eats our scraps of cheese and the fatty bits on the ham. I expect she's hungry all the time, with four growing babies to feed. Gabriel remains in his tree, sawing away and singing to himself a made up tune of made up words. I wonder if he has ever tried to saw off the branch he is sitting on. The saw is nearly as big as he is.

'Who lives in the cabin?' I ask Gabriel's mum.

'Moss's mother sleeps there when she visits. It's a granny cabin.'

What a lovely idea. I could live in a cabin like that. Fish from the stream, keep chooks. Heaven. Perhaps on my desert island I could eventually build a little shelter like that. I could have a garden of pebbles and shells, and cultivate coconuts and bananas and papayas, and oranges and lemons. I have always wanted a lemon tree. I love the smell of the leaves. Mum could pick a lemon and slice it straight into her gin and tonic. Except she won't be there. I'll cultivate a taste for gin, which I find in bottles on the wrecked ship, and wear the evening dress and toast her memory.

On the way home to St Ives – home to St Ives: that sounds so cool – a horse leaps over the stone hedge in front of the car, its lips curled to show yellow teeth. He screeches like a stallion in a movie. Another and another scramble over the dry-stone wall, tails and manes flying; eight beautiful animals, wild-eyed with excitement, run along in front of us. Their steaming bodies fill the lane as they jostle and skitter, their unshod hooves making muffled clunks on the road. Mum parks the car in a shallow lay-by and walks back to tell the farmer his horses have escaped. He appears, a large, red-cheeked man in braces, slaps his thighs and laughs, and lumbers after them. They have made their way onto a bridle path and are heading for Rosewall Hill and freedom. Now I know why it's called Horsetown.

A day of Darlings and marvels.

CHAPTER SEVENTEEN

MUM HAS TO go to the physiotherapist twice a week. She has been told not to do any gardening or decorating or hoovering. She's pretty fed up about it. She has good days and bad days; mostly bad days. She has a little machine with electrodes that she attaches to her skin and gives her muscles electric shocks – or that's what it looks like. The whisky supply is dwindling. She wouldn't last long on a desert island. She'd drink the barrel of ship's rum much too quickly.

I think the house looks fine the way it is, but she wants to put her own mark on it, like a cat squirting on its territory to keep out other cats. There are half stripped walls, with wallpaper torn off in places, like a map of the world. I like to see the layers of other people's taste – the flowery patterns and the geometric. We are going to have it all plain magnolia, or white, I expect. But at the moment she is incapable of doing anything at all except moaning, whimpering and drinking.

The pond is doing well and the water plants are settling in. There's a clump of miniature bamboo next to it.

I keep thinking about the family we met in Halsetown: a real family with a father and mother and three healthy children. How do they do it? Stay together? Is it because the husband and wife love each other and have never been unfaithful to each other? Is it because their children have nothing wrong with them?

It's because of me that a terrible strain was put on Mum and Daddy's marriage. Because of me being ill all the time and Mum having to stay at home to look after me. Daddy probably left because he's ashamed of having a sickly, puny, ugly, skinny daughter. Why did my family fall apart? It's not fair. I'm all the family Mum has got now. What will happen to her when I die? She'll have no one to look after her and make her cups of tea when she's sad and growing even more decrepit. She needs family too. (I always want to spell decrepit with a 'd' at the end. Decrepid sounds much better.)

I go to the library and try not to look guilty and criminal but it's difficult when you're a liar and a thief. I renew the nonexistent books again. I wonder how many times I am allowed to do that before they ask for them back. The library lady is very chatty. She asks me if my Mum is finding the books useful and I find myself lying even more.

'Oh yes, she's decorating the house and getting all sorts of ideas from one of the books, and she's building an enormous pond with a fountain and bridge, so the other book is very useful.'

'Really? How unusual.'

How am I going to get out of this? If only I had admitted that I had thrown them away at the beginning. But then, Mum would be horrified that I had gone to the funeral of someone I didn't know just because he was a Stevens. She doesn't understand me.

As I leave the library I notice a sign and an arrow – St Ives Archive. I think an archive is a collection of information and pictures, like a museum. I follow the arrow up some stairs lined with old photographs – sepia-toned prints of fishing boats and fishermen and gulls in the harbour. The harbour looked beautiful, full of masts and sails and gulls. There's a young woman working at a computer and an older man looking through a box file.

I squat to get my breath back. The woman comes to the reception desk and peers over the counter at me.

'Can I help you?'

I stand up. 'I hope so. I'm looking for a family.'

'What name?'

'Gussie, Augusta, actually.'

'Is that the name of the family you are looking for?'

How embarrassing: I'm so stupid. 'No. Sorry, Stevens.'

'Stevens? Oh yes, we have quite a few of those.'

'Yes, but do you have any who were car dealers in the area? He was my father's father. My grandfather.'

'What was his first name?'

I haven't the faintest idea.

'Er, I don't know.'

She sighs and shows me a series of box files on a shelf. An hour later she says the archive centre has to close. It's hopeless. There's no sign of a car dealer called Stevens.

At home I look in the *Yellow Pages* just in case there is still a car dealership with that name, but there isn't.

'Mum, what was Grandad Stevens' first name?'

'Don't know. Why?'

She is lying on her back on the carpet.

'Just wondered. What's for tea?'

'Nothing. Fish and chips maybe.'

'Yippee!'

Mum has been going out with Alistair on Friday evenings to the pub but he is in the Scillies on the cricket tour and he'll be gone all weekend. Mum is glum.

Last night I dreamed I was flying. I didn't have wings. It was like snorkelling in the sky. I could direct my flight with my hands, arms, legs and feet, like Batman, or Peter Pan. I was flying along at the same height above the ground as seagulls. It felt exhilarating, not cold or frightening, and even though I knew in the dream that I was not an expert flier I was enjoying the strange and wonderful sensation of speeding effortlessly through the sky and looking down at little yellow and green and brown fields, crows and gulls scattered like black and white confetti behind a tractor. And then I came to a coast of black jagged rocks, swooped down towards the wave-striped sea and woke up.

CHAPTER EIGHTEEN

OUR ADOLESCENT GULL is still wheezing and jumping up and down on the roof flapping his speckled wings. He wanders all over the roof, spends most of the time on his own, though one parent perches on the chimney top watching over him while the other parent is fishing for his supper, or is out having a good time.

I feel like that young gull: songless and ugly, unable to fly; totally dependent on my parent.

Mum and I are playing Scrabble. It's getting easier to beat her. She doesn't seem to care as much as she used to about losing. She always used to beat me.

I care.

In the town there are young gulls wandering around the alleyways and cobbled lanes looking bewildered and their anxious parents stand on the chimneys and shout. Most of the holidaymakers with school age children have gone home.

Our young gull has fallen into the garden, trying to fly, I suppose. One moment he's on the roof, next, he's on the grass. The parents kept swooping on us when we tried to rescue him, but eventually we managed to cover him in a blanket and pick him up. Mum carried him upstairs and put him out my window onto the roof. After half an hour of screaming in consternation the parents returned to the roof, no doubt amazed that he had managed to get back home on his own. He huddled by the chimney looking grumpy. I expect his mum has told him off for straying too close to the edge. She looks like a prim ballerina resting, and the big male ruffles his breast, wings and tail, sending small feathers floating away to become fluttering white butterflies. (Or that's what they look like to me without my glasses on.)

Summer seems to have gone. The waves are big and the northwesterly wind is cold. Clouds are grey and black with no gaps between them. No more sitting on the beach watching the sun go down.

Mum spends lots of time lying on the sofa or the floor. She also has headaches and hot flushes (power surges, she calls them). She's crumbling fast. I go to the pharmacy to pick up her prescription, taking a short cut through Trewyn Gardens where dead leaves are running like rats.

We don't see Eugene any more. He was our postie at Peregrine Cottage. We have a post-woman now. Her name is Leah. I wait for her every morning. She's very pretty with short purple hair.

Daddy has written to me at last. He's back from wherever and has sent me a ten pound note and a family tree, sort of: his father was called Hartley Stevens, born in St Ives, in 1900, and his mother, née – that means born – Molly Jackson, was born in Penzance. Daddy was named Jackson after her. He had no brothers or sisters and his father died when he was twenty-two and his mother when he was thirty, before I was born. No other information. Not very helpful really. More like a twig than a tree.

'Mum, may I telephone Daddy today?'

'What for?'

'To thank him for the money.'

She hangs around while I dial the number and I feel inhibited talking to him.

'Hi, Daddy, it's me.'

'Who is it? Is this my little honeybun? Gussie, how are you sweetie?' He makes me feel like I'm about five. I like it, rather.

'I got your letter Daddy. Thank you for the money and the information. But I thought you had cousins here. What are their names?'

'No Guss, not cousins, more like second cousins twice removed or something, very very distant relations. Almost out of sight.'

'Oh, but everyone is called Stevens here. Almost everyone. Apart from the ones called Symons and one or two others.'

'Sorry sweets, can't remember names. Gussie, got to go now, have to see a man about a movie.'

Yeah, yeah. You're a great help. Thanks for nothing, Daddy.

There's an invitation in the post. It's Brett's birthday on Sunday and we are both invited round to his house at lunchtime. Brilliant! What can I give him? I don't know his taste in anything. I know he likes birds. I think I'll get him a book token. As Mum says: You Can't Go Wrong with a Book Token.

Mum doesn't think she'll be well enough to drive to Brett's. Her back. She says it hurts too much. She *is* looking peaky, I admit. Brett lives in Carbis Bay, a suburb of St Ives, on the way to Peregrine Point. It's too far for me to walk.

'See how I feel after my next physio,' she says.

'When is that?'

'Friday.'

I make her a cup of peppermint tea and smile winningly.

That night I pray for her back to be better.

CHAPTER NINETEEN

WE'RE GOING! THANK you God.

Brett's parents live in a large bungalow just off the main road, with a distant view of the sea. They've got a barbie going, with burgers and sausages. Brett greets us and introduces us to his parents. His dad is a Science and Maths teacher and his mum is an English teacher, except she hasn't found work here yet. She is very pretty and much younger than my mum, but then everyone's mum is younger than mine. I've met his dad before at Hayle, birdwatching. He's young too, younger than Daddy and very Aussie with blond spiky hair, long baggy shorts and a loose T-shirt with UNI OF NSW splashed across the front. He looks a bit like the cricketer, Shane Warne. His name is Steve.

There's a garden with a few trees and hanging from each tree are loads of bird feeders. These people are seriously into birds: they provide peanuts, sunflower seeds, balls of fat and seeds, half coconut shells, apples, maize, the lot. You name it, they've got it. It's bird heaven: birdbath, bird table, pond for insects to evolve in – everything a little bird could chirp for. Brett's mum, she tells me to call her Hayley, says they only rented the house because it had a pond and a large garden.

The two boys I saw Brett with outside the library are here and two girls and various adults.

Brett has a tent pitched at the bottom of the garden where he sleeps sometimes, he says. How cool is that? He says he likes to look at the stars. There's an astronomy club at school and he and his two friends belong to it. He's been given a four-inch refractor telescope for his birthday. It's a large plastic tube on a sturdy tripod next to his tent. He shows me Saturn through it. That's amazing – to see a planet in daylight! I had no idea you could do that. He said he stayed up all night in the middle of August to watch the Perseids – a load of shooting stars.

'Where's Buddy?' I ask.

'Up there, watching us.'

Buddy sits in one of their tall trees and looks down on us. I wish he'd come down into the garden, but he's a bit wary of all the people, Brett says.

Bridget is nine and her sister, Siobhan (pronounced Shivawn) is a year older than me – she's thirteen. They are the sisters of Liam, one of Brett's friends. The other boy is Hugo.

Mum seems happy enough. She's drinking wine and talking to Brett's mum. The boys want to have a battle with water guns. You pump water through them and they are like water pistols only much much bigger. But Brett's dad says they can't with everyone in the garden and they'll have to wait until we go inside, but the sun is shining and it's really quite warm so we all stay outside eating and drinking and talking.

Brett gave me his curly smile and said thanks for the book token. I do like him.

Siobhan is pretty with long dark shiny hair and pierced ears, and wears a short pink skirt and a blue top and is rather quiet.

Her little sister is great fun. She wants to know all about me, where do I go to school and why don't I go to school, what is wrong with my heart, and will I have an operation? She never stops asking questions, like me when I was little. She tells me that she thinks in colours.

'What do you mean?'

'Well, pleasure is pink.'

'Okay.'

'Scarlet is a scolding.'

'Is it?'

'Pain is purple. I felt purple pain when I was stung by a weaver fish last year.'

'Stung by a weaver fish?'

'Yes, then the pain turned dark blue – that was agony.'

'What did you do?'

'A lifesaver on the beach carried me to their hut and put my foot in a bowl of hot water and the blue went away.'

'Ignore her, she's stupid,' says Siobhan.

Siobhan asks if I like Brett, and I say of course I do, he's cool. But she means, is he my boyfriend?

'Are you going out?'

'No way. We go birding together.'

'Birding?' She smiles in a sneering way and says he and the other boys are too young for her. I have decided I don't really like her much. She's in another universe. Alien. I prefer Bridget.

'Do you know a boy called Gabriel?' I ask Bridget.

'He's in my class. We're having one of his kittens. The black one. We're going to call him Spike.'

We lie down at the edge of the pond and I tell her about pond insect life.

Siobhan is hanging out with the adults, flirting with Brett's dad, flicking her hair back from her face and giggling.

Mum says she hates flirts. They steal other women's men. She says they have No Conception of Sisterhood. I think I understand what she means now.

The boys have joined Bridget and me by the pond and are listening to my account of the life cycle of a mosquito. Siobhan sidles over and lies next to Brett, her hip against his. I do believe he's blushing. Strewth! What does she think she is doing? Ohmygod!

Siobhan asks Brett to show her the tent, and he says Okay. They are going to the bottom of the garden, Siobhan in front, swaying her stupid hips in the short skirt, Brett following and I simply lie here, dumb-struck.

'Go on, Gussie, what happens next?' Bridget nudges me.

'The adult female mosquito finds a juicy fat victim like your sister, sucks her blood, injects her with malaria, yellow fever, elephantiasis or dengue fever, and she dies a long and painful death.'

CHAPTER TWENTY

I CAN'T HONESTLY say *I* enjoyed the party. Mum did though and she likes Brett's parents and I think they have persuaded her to let me go with them to the Scillies. However, I don't know if Brett still wants me to go. He might be under the spell of the ss – Shit-face Siobhan.

Mum has heard about this new trick to make her look younger. The girl who dyes her eyelashes told her about it. You put haemorrhoid cream under your eyes and it's supposed to reduce the bags. I am taking note of her beauty hints so I can be armed against the ss.

Mum says I don't need to worry just yet. Little does she know.

I do seriously need help with my appearance. My hair for a start. I can't do a thing with it. It's shapeless and lank.

'Mu-um.'

'Mmm?'

'I want my hair cut.'

'I'll trim it if you like.'

'No, I mean cut by a proper hairdresser.'

She stops dabbing at her eyes with the ointment and looks at me hard.

The hairdresser's is in a cobbled lane, tucked away. Sherie and Eve are the stylists and there is a beautician called Lulu. I am nervous.

Mum is having her roots done. She sits in one chair with gooey stuff all over her head, and I am in the next seat. This is worse than the dentist.

Sherie is talking about her horses. She lives in the country and has two.

She has just finished styling the white curly hair of an

elderly lady and she asks her if she would like Eve to walk up the hill with her to make sure she gets home.

'So,' says Sherie, 'how would you like it?' She shows me some hairstyle books. I would really like to look like Ginnie. Her hair is short and spiky, sort of punkish.

Sherie pulls my hair this way and that. She looks as though she would rather be grooming one of her horses. I look in the mirror. I look as though I would rather be fighting a bull. I find a photo of someone who looks similar to Ginnie and say this is how I want it to look.

Mum is deep into a crummy magazine about minor celebrities so I don't disturb her. Another elderly lady comes in and Mum starts talking to her. It's very busy here. The phone never stops ringing and people keep coming in and asking for appointments. Everyone knows everyone.

Eve's mum comes in and smokes a cigarette in the back part of the shop, which is separated from the front bit by flapping doors, like in a western. Mum flaps her arms and coughs extravagantly.

Here in the heart of town, the gulls are calling from the roofs; cars squeeze through the narrow street and negotiate the sharp corner; Radio Cornwall blares out pop music; hairdryers snarl; the telephone rings; there's constant laughter and chatter; people walk by and stare in past a huge glazed china Dalmation dog lying in the window among hairspray and shampoo bottles. Notices on the wall: STRESS BUSTER – BANG YOUR HEAD HERE. YOU DON'T HAVE TO BE CRAZY TO WORK HERE, BUT IT HELPS. Lulu runs up and down stairs with women who've come to have hair removed from various parts of their bodies or have their nails sharpened or something. All the staff are dedicated to make us feel better about ourselves. A lone man has his thin hair shaved off. It looks so much better, perhaps I should have mine shaved.

Snip snip snip. My hair on the floor all around me. Eve

shampoos me and massages my head. That is so good. I would like someone to massage my head every day. Then Sherie dries it with a hairdryer. She rubs some gel into my scalp and shapes my hair with her fingers, and cuts it some more.

Mum is still having her hair shampooed. When she emerges from the washbasin she notices me.

'Gussie? What have they done to you? You look great.'

In the mirror there is this small, thin person with a long neck and shining sticking-up hair, more like Dennis the Menace than Ginnie, but it's cool. Sherie is pleased with the result and Lulu and Eve admire it too.

I'm not sure I can get my England cap over my hair without flattening it.

I could cope with this hairstyle on a desert island. Use gull's egg-white to glue it into place.

The elderly lady has had her white curls curled tighter. They look like white Brussels sprouts. As Eve shows her out the door she says, 'Goodbye Mrs Stevens. See you next week.'

Not another Stevens! They're everywhere. But which ones are my Stevenses?

I've given up reading *Robinson Crusoe*. I know he meets Man Friday, but when for goodness sake? I'm on page 150 and he hasn't appeared yet. And he's never short of food or water, and he has fire, weapons, shelter, cats, dogs, a parrot that talks, and goats. If he suddenly discovered a McDonalds or an Indian take-away on the far beach, I wouldn't be surprised.

There's a very good Indian take-away next to the hairdressers. It's called Ruby Murries. It's rhyming slang – Ruby Murry – Curry. They deliver. We usually have something from them once a week. Would they deliver on my desert island?

CHAPTER TWENTY-ONE

BRETT LIKES MY hair. We meet by chance in the library.

'Strewth! You look rippa, Guss,' is what he says.

Luckily the chatty woman isn't at the desk today to enquire about home improvements.

'Gussie, what are you singing?' Mum shouts from the bathroom.

'*Waltzing Mathilda.*' I sing it again for her benefit – 'Waltzing Mathilda, waltzing Mathilda, who'll go a waltzing...?'

'Okay, okay I thought it sounded familiar.'

CHAPTER TWENTY-TWO

THE CONTACT SHEETS of the photographs I made in Shamrock Lodge arrived today. I like the ones with the stripes of light and shade, the men concentrating on their domino game. I will definitely do some more at the other lodges. Ages ago Dad gave me a load of out of date black and white film, which he says is still absolutely okay. I am suddenly filled with enthusiasm. The pictures of the washing line aren't bad either.

In the *Times and Echo* there's a piece about an arts festival in St Ives. There will be poetry readings, novelists reading, writing workshops, and the artists' studios will be open to the public.

Cool, I mean, rippa, I'll get lots of good photographs.

At the moment I'm trying to capture the image of a huge yellow moth that is beating against the glass roof-light in my room. It sounds like an overflow pipe discharging a fast trickle of water. I feel so sorry for it I switch off the light. It works: I have stopped the moth's running water imitation.

Mum has found an odd job man to do things in the house. She found him in the newsagent's window. He's overweight and smells of butter and cigarettes and is called Arnold. Apart from that he's very nice. He's fixed the cat-flap in the front door, built some bookshelves in the sitting room and is having a cup of tea with Mum and me. He says he does gardening too. He and his wife came here from Birmingham four years ago and they both do several jobs – waiting and bar work in the summer season and anything that comes along in the winter months. He worked for British Telecom before and can put his hand to most things around a house.

He has very long ear lobes with large holes in as if he's

worn earrings that damaged his ears or someone caught hold of the earrings and yanked them hard (perhaps I could do that to ss?). He reminds me of Babar the Elephant. It's that placid expression.

I had all the Babar books when I was little, some in French or Spanish, depending on where we were when they were bought for me. I think Mum probably made up the stories when she read to me at bedtime because I don't think she speaks Spanish or French. But Babar wasn't my favourite bedtime read. I always needed *Winnie the Pooh* when I was really ill or miserable or couldn't get to sleep. My favourite story was 'Piglet is Entirely Surrounded by Water', because it's a long story told from various points of view – Piglet's, Pooh's and Christopher Robin's, and Mum enjoyed reading it. Come to think of it, Piglet sends off a message in the bottle. I could do that on my desert island. I could also write a message in the sand. sos. What does that stand for, apart from Save Our Sausages?

'Not at school?' Arnold says.

'She's getting over an operation,' explains Mum, and thankfully doesn't go into the sordid details of my medical history. I always get embarrassed when she tells people about my heart. I would rather no one knew, and treated me like a normal person, not a disabled one. I hate that sad dreamy look of understanding and sympathy that people put on when I am talked about. My mind is normal, for goodness sake; my brain is no different from any other twelve-year old's.

I desperately want to ask about the damage to his ears. Perhaps he was in deepest darkest Brazil, involved in some strange tribal ritual just to be friendly. Weird things do happen to people who are only trying to be polite or to fit in. I can't think of any at the moment, but I'm sure I will.

I suppose it's like those metal neck rings that stretch your neck that some women in Africa have to wear, because it's the local custom.

Or female circumcision. Yuk. Don't even want to think about that.

Why are girls suddenly getting tattoos? You can't go back on 'I love Kevin', can you, when you fall out of love with him and love Fred? You can't cross out Kevin and write Fred. You'd have to fall in love with some boy with a name of equal length, like Brian, or Jason, or the scar would show. No way could you tattoo Joe or Bill or Brett. It would be more sensible to have a shortened version like Kev tattooed, then you could add to it later, when necessary, when you had a boyfriend with a long name, then there'd be no visible scar tissue.

Speaking of which – my own scar is itching like mad.

Must find out to say that in Strine – like billy-o, possibly.

CHAPTER TWENTY-THREE

SHORE SHELTER. SEVERAL old men. I first make a photo of the wall where no men are sitting. NO SWEARING ALLOWED is written large on a notice board. Old paintings and faded photographs of men and boys fishing in boats and unloading fish in the harbour line the walls.

'Are women allowed to join the lodge?'

'If they want. But they all be 'ome making pasties for us' dinners.'

'How do you make a pasty?' I ask Mr Perkin.

'You'll 'ave to ask the wife.'

'I do the cooking in our house,' says a thin man, tamping down the tobacco in his pipe and lighting it with a match.

'So do you know the recipe for pasties?' I ask, all the time shooting pictures as they laugh and chat.

'I buy short pastry from Co-op like, roll it out, cut into rounds with a plate. Then you get the filling ready.' He fiddles with the pipe and clears his throat. 'Chop up potato and a bit of steak and onion; mix it in a bowl with a little bit of water and with a bit of salt and pepper – I like lots of pepper.

'Put the mix on half the circle and fold it over like. Then you press the edges together and crimp them, like that.'

He shows me how to crimp, pressing his blunt fingers on the edge of the table.

'Bake in the oven for about an hour.'

'You forgot to prick 'oles to let the steam out,' says another man.

'Oh 'es, proper job,' says the cook, and lights his pipe yet again.

'My 'oman puts in turnip as well as potato,' says a man with a stick.

'You'm spoilt rotten, you are.' They all laugh and the turnip man looks amused and pleased.

Another man says they used to eat sheep's heads when he was a boy. Yuk.

'I was brought up on spuds and bread. If you had a meal, even if it was a sheep's head boiled in broth: "Have a maw" the old people didn't call it a slice of bread then – "that'll help fill up the crevices." Even if you had a salt herring and potatoes boiled in their jackets: Have a maw to fill up the holes.'

I shoot some more film in Rose Shelter too. There the men are playing euchre, a card game. But the light has gone flat and dull and the pictures I see through the viewfinder are not very exciting. It's smoky in here so I don't last long. But as I go to leave one of the men says, 'Local maid, are you, my flower?'

'I'm a Stevens.'

'News gets around.'

'I'm Augusta. My dad is Jackson Stevens.'

The men all look at each other.

'Oh ah, Jackson Stevens, eh?

'That be Hartley's boy.'

'Yes, Hartley Stevens was my grandfather.'

'Never mind cheel', never mind.'

'What do you mean?'

'Oh nothing, only 'e were a bit wild, 'e were.' The old men laugh loud.

''Es, 'e paid for it though. Never mind them, my flower.' A bent over man, who looks about a hundred, winks at me.

I feel a sort of reflected guilt and shame, even though I don't know what my father's father did that was wild.

'What did he do exactly?'

'Oh, some sort of skulduggery. What was 'e accused of, Tom?'

'Fiddled with car milometers, I heard.'

'No, it were something about property. Always buying and selling land, 'Artley were.'

''Es, fingers in many pies, 'es.'

''E left town after. Took wife and boy away.'

Oh dear, I am taking after my Grandfather Hartley, lies and skulduggery. I feel myself go hot around the neck and face.

'There's only Dad left now, anyway. His parents both died years ago.'

'Never mind, my flower. Plenty of 'onest Stevenses left here, any'ow,' says the friendly one.

''Artley's sister – what was her name?' said the bent-over one.

'Fay. 'Es, Fay, 'andsome she were. Red hair. 'Es, I courted she, but she wouldn't 'ave I. Din' want no fisherman.'

'Din' want a scrawny fool you mean.' The old men are chuckling and coughing.

'Married a big man, Fay did, not from 'ere, foreigner.'

'Get on with the game, will you,' says the thin one as he shuffles the cards.

I have to get out into the fresh air. The smoke is too much for me. Anyway, it's getting late. Mum will be wondering where I am.

I wish I could have stayed and found out more.

CHAPTER TWENTY-FOUR

BAD NEWS. I bump into Bridget with her mum in Woolies. Her mum is in the sheets and towels aisle. Bridget and I shovel sweets into little paper bags – I go for the large flat toffees and she likes the cola sweets – and she tells me Brett has been to their house after school every day this week.

To see Liam? I don't think so.

Bridget says her sister has had her belly-button pierced. Not only that, she has started to wear a padded uplift bra. She hangs around with Liam and Brett all the time and ignores Bridget or is horrible to her.

'She's a total pain in the neck.'

'Purple or blue?'

'Blue, midnight blue.'

I totally agree.

I am back at the archive with my new information. When I recover my breath I say, 'I want to find out more about my father's family. My grandfather was Hartley Stevens, born 1900. He died though. But he had a sister, Fay.'

The woman shows me a box file full of Stevenses. No sign of any Hartleys or Fays but I find a long list of family nicknames including some lovely ones and some rather rude ones: Halibut Dick; Edwin Gull; Joe Powerful; Dick Salt; George Tealeaves; Georgie Pupteen; Georgie Happy; Willy Sailor; Polly Wassey; Captain Starve Guts; Tilly Toots; Bessie Wet Tits (seriously, I'm not joking).

As I give up and go to leave my eye is drawn by one of the framed photographs on the stairs. It's a close up of two men mending a fishing net on Smeaton's Pier, their backs to the camera. There is a signature – Amos H Stevens, and a date – 1927.

I go back to the desk and ask for information on Amos H Stevens, photographer.

'Oh yes, there's a book somewhere. Try over there.'

I eventually find the right book – *The Good Old Days* – photographs and paintings of the town in years gone by. I look in the index and there he is, his name: Amos Hartley Stevens.

I go to the page and find what I am looking for: Amos Hartley Stevens, born 1880, Street an Garrow, St Ives. Proprietor, St Ives Photographic Studio, Fore Street, St Ives. My grandfather Hartley was born in 1900, so this must have been his father – my great-grandfather. A real professional photographer! Photography must be in my genes.

No news from Brett about the Scillies. I haven't seen him for ages.

I have never felt so much hatred for another person – ss I mean, obviously.

VERBS *Hate, detest, loath, abhor, execrate, abominate, hold in abomination, take an aversion to, shudder at, utterly detest, not stand the sight of, not stand, not stomach, scorn, despise, dislike.*

Yes, all of those.

It isn't fair that some girls are pretty and some aren't ever going to be, no matter what they do to themselves. I still like my new haircut of course, but underneath it I am still the same ugly geek. No amount of piercing or short skirts will change the way I feel about myself or other people feel about me. Life is not fair. My teeth aren't white or straight. My legs are weedy, my fingers are clubbed – because of my heart. My skin is blue, my tits and hips nonexistent. At least I haven't got hairy toes or nostrils.

My jealousy is a poisonous acid green. It must show, surely? Jealousy is a terrible curse.

'Gussie, what is wrong with you?'

'What? Why?'

'You look so grumpy, Guss.'

'I'm nearly a teenager, I'm supposed to be grumpy.'

Even the cats are discriminating against me. They have taken to exploration. Having once taken the plunge to do a recce of the garden, they spend all their time outside, fraternising with the neighbourhood cats.

I sit in the window and try to take my mind off my problems by immersing myself in watching the birds and making notes, drawing sketches of the gulls.

I am also becoming more literate – learning a new word every day. I simply open the dictionary at any page and pick a word I haven't heard of before. I'll try and use the word on the day I learn it, to make sure I remember it. Today's word is '*immiseration – a progressive impoverishment or degradation.*' Huh, that's where I'm headed.

It reminds me of *The Dice Man* – a book Daddy was once keen on. Every day you make a list of things to do, give each a number, throw the dice and whatever number comes up, you do that thing – it could be rob a bank or move to Australia, become a gun runner or take up karate. Maybe that's how he came to run off with TLE. He threw a dice and her number came up.

List of things I could do about ss:

1. Ignore her.
2. Tell her what I think of her.
3. Get her little sister Bridget to give her a note ostensibly from Brett, but written by me, telling her he doesn't fancy her. (Last time I tried forging a signature it was a total failure. I went off Religious Education when I was eight and wrote a note to the teacher saying, 'Please may Augusta be excused lessons as she is not relijus.')

4. Become a nun.
5. Be really really nice to her so she feels guilty.
6. Wear an even shorter skirt than hers, get a long dark wig, false eyelashes and stuff oranges up my T-shirt.

Where's the dice?
Also, my family problem. Do I:

1. Tell Mum about my famous antecedent?
2. Tell Daddy?
3. Keep quiet about what I have found out?
4. Go on with the search for living relations?
5. Forget all about family?
6. Ask Brett's advice?

Still can't find a dice – or is it die? Why is life so complicated? And language. It's so easy to seem a complete dork by saying the wrong thing. Can't think how to bring immiseration into the conversation either.

CHAPTER TWENTY-FIVE

MUM AND I are revisiting Paradise Park. She might not enjoy birding, but for some reason she likes coming here. It is peaceful and relaxing, which must be good, and one of the falconers is Rather a Hunk, she says.

The group of flamingos are as usual standing on one leg, trying to tie their necks in knots. I always imagined them to be taller than they are, and pinker. More pink, that should be.

We stroke Houdini, an elderly female penguin, named after the famous escape artist because she kept getting out when she was first rescued. Her back feathers feel like the pelt of a warm-blooded animal. She was hand reared and really enjoys being touched. She pushes against your hand, like a cat.

I really want to see the keas, but they've been moved away from the Australian section, where you could get up to the wire and almost touch them, and look into their eyes, and put into a huge aviary with lots of different sorts of parrots, where we can't get close. I want to talk to them and watch their reactions. They are particularly intelligent and clever at solving problems – like getting through all sorts of obstacles to reach food. They are notorious at working together to peck and peel off rubber seals on tourist car windows to get at food inside. I'd like to find a good book about keas. Their bronze feathers look like scales or coats of armour, with red underneath the wings. Instead of walking they hop along the ground. In the wild they live on mountaintops on the South Island, of New Zealand. That's somewhere I would love to go, but I don't suppose I'll have time.

Knowing you are probably going to die in a year or two is like waiting for a train with people you really like seeing you off, and you know you aren't going to see them ever again. You have so much you want to say to them and the train is due in any moment. There's so little time. You try to find the right words but your loved ones are left on the platform not knowing what it is you really needed to say. And I suppose it's the same for them. What can they possibly say?

CHAPTER TWENTY-SIX

I HAD A terrible dream last night: I had had my heart and lung transplant and the surgeon had forgotten to stitch up the incision so my chest was open, and blood glued the sheet to the edges of the wound. I woke in a sweat, my heart pounding like mad.

I have had an awful feeling all day, as if I have taken out the plug in the bath and my body is being sucked down with the disappearing water, dragged down.

I watch a red-headed fly wash its hands and arms very thoroughly like a surgeon scrubbing up. It does the same thing to its back legs.

Mum says I don't look too good: bags under the eyes and mauve lips, and she takes my temperature, makes me Horlicks and biscuits as a treat before Rena Wooflie and I have an early night – 8pm! With a hot water bottle.

'Do you want a story?'

'Please. Winnie the Pooh.'

'Which one?'

'You choose.'

She reads me 'A Pooh Party', where Pooh gets pencils marked HB for Helpful Bear, and pencils marked BB for Brave Bear. I forget how to say goodnight to Rena Wooflie in Swahili. I'm vaguely aware of a cool hand on my forehead. Mum opens the window and switches off the lamp.

CHAPTER TWENTY-SEVEN

IN THE SECOND-HAND book shop there's a very good Natural History section. I have managed to buy a battered copy of *The Natural History of Selborne* and a 1937 copy of *The Charm of Birds* by Grey of Fallodon, owned in 1937 by a Marjorie Phyllis Crighton. I might give the second one to Brett. This is a lesson on taming robins:

> First throw breadcrumbs on the ground. Then a meal-worm. Robins love them. Then place an open metal box, like a sweetie tin, on the ground, with meal-worms in it. When the bird is accustomed to this, kneel down and place the tin in an open hand, flat to the ground, with fingers sticking out in front of the tin. The robin will eventually stand on your fingers and feed from the tin. This might take time. Then do away with the tin and place some meal-worms on the hand. A robin will risk his life for a meal-worm. The final stage is to stand up with meal-worms on the open palm. In hard weather the whole process will take only two or three days. Once the robin is confident that you won't harm him, he'll come in fair weather when other food is plentiful.

I think Brett could tame any wild creature.

I've also found this old book for 50p in the second-hand bookshop. *Secrets of Bird Life*, by HA Gilbert and Arthur Brook, published by Arrowsmith in 1924. It was once owned by GT Pettit, aged thirteen. He had very beautiful neat handwriting. My handwriting is crap. Perhaps I should be a doctor. There is an interesting description of raven babies:

The hen raven sits close by and croons to her very ugly babies, who have huge stomachs and enormous maws, which they open whenever they hear a noise or when a shadow passes over them. When they all open their beaks together it looks like a nest full of violets has suddenly bloomed as their throats and mouths are a brilliant mauve.

What a lovely idea! Baby birds gaping like a bunch of violets. Perhaps I could put that in a poem.

Brett and Siobhan. Are they 'going out'? Well, frankly my dear, I don't give a damn.

Charlie, Flo and Rambo are due for their flu booster jabs so Mum is going to get the vet to visit and give them anti flea injections at the same time. We do groom the cats every day. When the flea comb is sharply tapped on the garden table the cats come running. Charlie is always the first and most demanding. Fleas seem to go for her white throat, like miniature vampires. Flo wants to be combed but then as you go to do it she changes her mind and runs away. She knows it's good for her but feels it is beneath her dignity for someone else to do her scratching for her. Rambo will take any amount of combing, can't get enough of it. He always has most fleas on his thighs or haunches. He's a big cat and has much thicker, coarser fur than the other two, so has more fleas. It's easy to catch them in the fine teeth of the comb but more difficult to actually squash them, especially the small black ones. I find it very satisfying to pop the large pale juicy ones. Afterward you have to really scrub your fingernails though.

I wonder why cats' fur smells so woody and leafy and clean? Surely they should smell fishy or meaty, because they clean themselves with saliva from mouths that have eaten flesh.

Brett is here. His mum and mine are meeting for coffee later this morning. No doubt for Mum to give her the low-down on my condition and what to do in a crisis etc. I'll have the hospital bleeper on me anyway. And it's good that Alistair will be on the Scillies at the same time as me.

I show Brett *Secrets of Bird Life* and give him the robin book. He lends me a book about Australian birds.

I would love to see an Australian bower bird. They all collect objects to decorate their nests, a bit like Mum collecting old lace tablecloths and linen pillowcases, to make the house look beautiful. Bower birds do it to attract a mate.

I collect feathers and shells and old nests and driftwood – natural objects to decorate my room. Am I doing it to attract a mate? I found out about bower birds from a book on Australian birds in the library.

Satin Bower Bird – the adult male is a glossy blue-black with lilac blue eyes. The female and the immatures are a dull green, banded below. Its bower is made of twigs arranged into a short avenue 30 cm high on a platform of knitted twigs. He paints it with saliva and chewed plants, sometimes using a twig as paint brush. He decorates the platform with yellow and blue things like leaves and straw. He might even steal his neighbour's ornaments and wreck his bower. He is a good mimic too. One Great Bower Bird, whose nest was near a construction site, was heard displaying by mimicking construction noises. Other bower birds decorate their bowers with shells and feathers and anything blue and white.

Mum gets all sorts of lovely things at car boot sales. She loves other people's junk. Most of our furniture and china is second-hand. She found a crystal chandelier once, and we have odd chairs from the fifties and sixties and nothing matches, but it all looks good together. She enjoys making a house look interesting. I suppose it's like playing with a dolls' house only bigger and more expensive.

Brett says he's really looking forward to going to the Scillies. His mum booked two rooms in a hotel on St Mary's ages ago, and as they are twin rooms, they can fit me in. We are getting there by helicopter from Penzance. Mum isn't going. I think she regrets saying she didn't want to go but someone has to stay and look after the cats. Brett and I mooch in the attic all morning, reading and watching the gulls, and talking.

He makes the observation that some flies – not fruit flies or bluebottles, but medium-sized silent flies – know how to make a right angle turn. They travel in squares up to the ceiling, they really do. He's so clever. I'd never noticed that before.

Bluebottles, when they are trapped, travel in straight lines from one end of their prison, a room, say, to the other. If you time it right, when they are about to turn back you can open a window or door in their path and they get out without you having to resort to a fly swat.

Flies, mosquitoes and cat fleas are the only creatures I ever try to kill.

'How's Buddy?'

'Beaut. Yeah, he's beaut, thanks. Finds food for himself mostly, just comes to see us for a stroke and a chat. Dad's working and I'm at school, so it's just as well he's learned to be independent. Mum's a bit scared of that powerful beak.'

'Seen any good meteors lately?'

'Na, it's been too cloudy.'

'I really like your mum.'

'Yeah, she's cool, for a mother. So's yours.'

'Is she? She's old of course, but yeah, she's not so bad, I suppose. How's Siobhan?' Shit, I didn't mean to mention her.

'Yeah, she's cool.' He is blushing.

Shit shit shit.

And he didn't notice my bower decorations – so he isn't attracted to me. I'll have to get more. More blue things and white things. Or give up.

I don't believe it – I'm mooching along the wharf, looking for things to photograph when I see ss in the amusement arcade. She's hanging on the arm of Hugo, who is all over her. What a slag!

I wonder if Brett knows about his so called best friend and his girlfriend? He'd be so upset. They are so intent on mauling each other and blowing smoke in each other's faces they don't notice me. In future I shall refer to her as sss.

CHAPTER TWENTY-EIGHT

IT'S HALF TERM, and a family has arrived next door. Through the wall we hear them shouting at each other and running up and down the stairs. We meet in the garden. There are two girls called Daisy and Grace, who are fourteen and eleven. Grace wants to see my room and she likes cats.

Daisy is miserable because she wanted to be in London this Christmas to go to parties. She says she hates St Ives. There's nothing to do, nowhere to go. They live in Dulwich and this is their holiday home.

I am getting ready to go to the Scillies and only have time to say hello. But they will be here at Christmas.

A slow mist covers the bay like a gauzy chiffon scarf. Will it be too foggy for the helicopter to fly? Mum drives me to the heliport. Brett and his mum and dad are there already, so is Alistair. There are a couple of other birdwatchers I recognise from Hayle, who are also going on the trip. I have my lightweight backpack of clothes, toothbrush etc and binoculars. I'm so excited.

In a separate room, like a mini departure lounge, we watch a safety video of people calmly putting on lifebelts while smiling inanely at their children. As if! Why don't we all wear our lifebelts before we get on the helicopter so if there's a crash into the sea, we'll be prepared. I'll never be able to get it out from under the seat and remember how to tie the thing on before we crash.

Anyway, I'd die of hypothermia in the first ten minutes of being in the sea, even if I floated, so I think I'd rather not bother with trying to find the thing, tying ribbons, pulling red tags, and blowing whistles and all that crap. Forget it. If I die on a journey, so be it. Better to be travelling than sitting still. That sounds like the sort of thing my Grandpop would have said, but I don't think he did. Perhaps it's a Zen thing.

We show our boarding cards and walk out to the helicopter. I hold on to my hat, fearful of the whirling blades, warm air from the engines blowing into our faces. My imagination has the blades flying off and decapitating all of us. Brett sits next to his dad and his mum sits next to me behind them in the back seat.

I wave to Mum out the window. Goodbye little Mum, you look so small and sad.

It's so noisy we can't hear ourselves speak. Penzance a miniature town below, the blue swimming pool on the seafront, the tiny harbour of Mousehole. We fly through wispy cloud and into blueness, 500 feet above the sea. A lighthouse on a rock, lonely in the big sea. Our first sight of the islands, low, rusty with bracken, white sand edges, islets and black rocks. Turquoise shallow water you can see through to the pebbles and sand below. Little jigsaw fields and greenhouses, farm buildings and granite cottages. A full washing line in the middle of a field. White doves like breadcrumbs on a roof. Lighthouses, cows, empty white beaches. A smooth landing on a perfect desert island.

We drop off our luggage at the hotel and go out for lunch of crab sandwiches in a café with a view of the working harbour. We learn that there haven't been any rare birds seen on the islands yet this year. It's a bit early for migrant stragglers lost in the Atlantic.

I don't care if we don't see any birds at all: I am on a beautiful desert island with Brett. I'm in Paradise.

We're on a red boat named *Seahorse*. The boatman is a high-cheeked youth of about twenty with curly yellow hair tied back on the nape of his tanned neck. His dog, yellow and sleek with a long kind face and gentle eyes, hangs around on the pier until the boat sails then jumps on board and wanders around on deck gazing lovingly at his master whenever he sees him. We spot lots of shag and cormorants, standing on a big rock hanging out their wings to dry. A pair of sandwich terns with their little forked tails spread fly overhead – Squeak, squeak, squeak.

At the landing slipway of St Agnes the handsome boatman jumps off and makes fast the ropes. We disembark and head for the Turk's Head, which is very close, and I only have to stop a few times. Brett waits for me while his parents go ahead. When we get there, they have mugs of hot chocolate waiting for us and we sit in sunshine on picnic benches overlooking a rocky little beach. It's so quiet. No cars.

We all eat pasties and I tell Brett's mum the recipe I got from the old man in the fisherman's lodge. Hayley says they are bit like mutton pies, a popular Australian dish. Alistair is going off with other birders to the other end of the island.

We are about to leave the pub when Brett points out a young herring gull struggling in shallow water. It seems to have become entangled in a child's crab line; orange nylon wrapped around its head, the square reel dragging in the water. It's in real trouble.

'I'll go and help it,' I say, but Hayley forbids me to step in the water.

'No way are you going in there. It's freezing, Guss,' she says, 'Your mother would never forgive me if you caught a chill.'

Brett and his dad walk down the slipway, take off their flip flops and paddle out to the bird, which struggles to fly off but cannot. Brett takes off his T-shirt and throws it over the gull's head to quieten it and to stop it stabbing them, but it attempts to escape and somehow Brett ends up completely immersed in water. They eventually cut it free with a penknife and unwrap the string from the bird's neck. It flies off spraying water over the already soaked pair of rescuers. A loud hurray and applause from me, Hayley, and the other customers of the Turk's Head. My hero! My sodden hero. Luckily he's wearing those quick drying shorts like surfers wear.

We walk along a little path and cross the sand-spit, the Bar, to the isle of Gugh, pronounced Gew, where there are two strange, Dutch-looking houses with wavy roofs, and a shipwrecked fishing boat, rusty, high and dry.

Long strings of khaki weed are wrapped around pink boulders, like badly tied parcels. On the tide line I look for little yellow periwinkle shells and their brother brown shells. I find a lost fishing lure: a staring blue eye, very real looking, with a hairy tail, fish hook hidden. I'm glad I didn't stand on it. I spot bright blue strands of cord a bower bird would die for. The sand is pimpled with limpet shells. There's no sound except little waves swishing and dragging at the sand. Oystercatchers and a stately grey heron silently fish the rock pools.

We gather together our discovered treasures – a piece of driftwood shaped a little bit like the hull of a boat, a blue polythene bag, orange string, a little square of wave-worn wood, and Brett and his dad build a little sailing boat with the blue eye as figurehead. They even make a keel, filling the polythene bag with water to weigh it down. It's ace.

We try it out in a rock pool to make sure it doesn't sink and then Brett and I launch it properly into the sea.

'I name this ship the *Valiant Augusta*. God bless her and all who sail in her.' He pushes the fragile craft into the gentle waves and we watch as she bobs in the shallows.

We walk by an inland pool where a heron stands on a grassy islet, his neck and shoulders hunched like our young herring gull. Do birds get bored I wonder?

The cropped grass we tread is not grass at all, but chamomile, and smells like herbal tea, but fresher. On the white sand beach are bands of pink boulders and blackened dead stalks of seaweed dragged by the sea from the deep. At the edge of the beach marram grass curls like waves over low stone hedges. There's no time to see all the island and anyway I'm tired. I sit down and rest after every twenty metres or so. Brett stops too, and we look through our binoculars at the oystercatchers and sea birds. We spot curlew, sandpiper and dunlin, their little legs moving so fast they look like clockwork toys. Turnstones are busy searching for sand hoppers on the strand line. No puffins. They breed in burrows on the small islands of Scilly Rock and Men-a-vaur off St Agnes between spring and July. I know this because I bought a book on the Scillies birds.

Brett's mum and dad are walking along together holding hands. If only that was my mum and daddy.

Brett and I lie back, our rucksacks sheltering us from the cool breeze, the sun on our heads.

I could stay here forever. I could die right now, I'm so happy.

We get the last boat back to St Mary's in the fading purple light, the stars appearing one by one, and Brett points them out to me and tells me their names, which I immediately forget, and as we land at the pier Brett goes first onto the granite steps and reaches out his hand to me to help me. I take it and smile at him and in the lamplight I see his curly smile and I am no longer shipwrecked, I am flying, soaring in a warm blue clear sky.

Hayley and I are sharing a room and Brett and his dad are sharing another. She's so thoughtful. Lets me use the bathroom first and fills my hot water bottle from the kettle and puts it in my bed. I like it really hot. She's reading *Middlemarch* and is surprised when I tell her I've read it.

She asks if we did it at school and when I say no, she says, 'You're very well read for a girl your age.'

'I've missed lots of school, so I read a lot.'

'You're an autodidact.'

'A what?'

'Self-taught. It means self-taught.'

I go scarlet – well, violet probably, as the red blush would mix with the blue. It never occurred to me that there were people who taught themselves. I thought you had to have teachers.

It's Sunday and we're off to visit Tresco on another boat. The sea's choppier today but it's only a short trip, shorter than to St Agnes. The boatman is called Frazer and he's lived on Scilly all his life. There's one pub, the New Inn, just around the corner from where we land, and all the boat's passengers seem to be heading there past granite cottages with little front gardens full of strange exotic plants, monster Aloes and Agaves, with hand painted signs at the gates – LOBSTERS FOR SALE or FRESH CRABMEAT. Huge juicy aeoniums grow from cracks in the stone hedges while strange leafless belladonna lilies (Naked Ladies, they call them here), with pink stems and bright pink flowers, grow from the base.

A sleek black cat runs along the sandy path in front of us and leads us to the pub garden, where he climbs up into a palm tree and stares down at us.

My hot prawn baguette is perfect. A thrush lands on the table and I feed him crumbs. Immediately, sparrows surround me and I have to feed them too.

We explore Tresco Abbey garden, where bumblebees heavy with nectar tumble drunkenly from towering echium, perfect blue tower-block cities for white butterflies and honey bees to gather nectar. Huge heads of pink king protea are feeding grounds for peacock butterflies, who fold and unfold their wings in an ecstasy of sweetness. It is surely the Garden of Eden. Hayley's into flowers and plants. She knows all the Latin names.

There's even a place where old ships' figureheads are

displayed: Valhalla, it's called, and Brett's dad takes loads of photographs. I haven't brought my camera as it is too heavy to cart around all over the place.

I buy postcards at the shop to remind me of the islands, but I won't ever forget, anyway.

It's a shame Mum isn't here; she'd love it.

Brett and I wander off across the helicopter landing-pad (it doesn't come on Sundays), stop to watch three Brent Geese bending their strong necks to the grass, then find ourselves in a field of silver logs. Parasol mushrooms are growing here. They are exactly like the name; the young ones like closed parasols and the open ones like open parasols. Fairies should be sitting on them. (I keep quiet about fairies; he'll think it a bit girlie.) They are supposed to be delicious, Parasol mushrooms, not fairies, but we don't pick them as we're eating at the New Inn before we catch the boat back to St Mary's.

The field is tussocky with heather and moss and the smells of herbs and honeysuckle.

We lean out of the wind against a silver log, its bark peeled off and curled up like a shed snake skin, bees buzzing and butterflies flickering their pretty wings around us, when suddenly there's a terrific whirring whistling, and three swans fly low, close above us, heading for the lake next to the gardens.

'Did you know the Queen owns all the swans in England?'

'She doesn't, does she?'

It makes me feel good to be able to tell him something he doesn't know about birds.

I tell Brett about my desert island fantasy and he agrees this place would be ideal. He's read *Swiss Family Robinson* and we agree that it's a ridiculous story. The shipwrecked family happen to have been on a ship equipped with everything to build a new settlement. So there are no obstacles for them; they have everything they could possibly want. Also, the father is totally pompous and self important and can build anything, including a bridge. If I had been his wife or daughter I would have wanted to strangle him.

Brett's been to islands in the Great Barrier Reef including Heron Island, which is very hot and humid and stinks of guana, that's bird shit, because of the thousands of Sooty Terns nesting in every bush and tree. You can look right into the nests and watch the young. You have to look out for muttonbirds as they are quite likely to fly bang into you in the dark as they aren't any good at landing. They nest in burrows in the sand.

'Oh, it sounds wonderful,' I say, but he says there are sharks and box jellyfish and other mortal dangers and he prefers it here.

I tell him about Kenya and my winters there when I was little: vervet monkeys on the roof, the giant butterflies and snorkelling. Then somehow I begin to tell Brett about my quest, the search for my roots, my Cornish family history. He can't understand why Mum is against it. He's dead impressed about my great-grandfather being a famous photographer.

I also tell him what the men in the lodge said about my Grandfather Stevens.

'Shall I tell Mum?'

'What's there to lose, Guss? She won't bite you.'

'Yeah, but she really doesn't want to know. I feel as if I am being... I don't know... disloyal to her.'

'Crap. I'll get Ma to have a talk with her.'

'No! Thanks, no. I'll sort it.'

'You sure?'

'Yes, I'll talk to her.'

'No worries,' he says and smiles curlily. Is there such a word? There should be.

In my mind I transform Grandad Stevens into a pirate with a black eye patch – skulduggery sounds so much more exciting and adventurous than fraud, which is only a posh word for theft and lying.

CHAPTER TWENTY-NINE

WE HAVE TO wait for a couple of hours at St Mary's airport as fog cover at Penzance delays flights, so we have bacon rolls and hot drinks at the café.

At the next table there's a family with three children. The children are dressed in school uniform, even the little boy, who is about four – who wears grey shorts, white shirt, red and white striped tie. He looks so cute. He's carrying a toy monkey, floppy and brown and wearing checked pyjamas. I ask him if he takes Monkey to school. He nods. His mum says, 'Oh yes, last year Monkey got a report, his attendance was so good.'

A group of excited schoolchildren from the Scillies are heading off to Plymouth to see a production of *Joseph and the Amazing Technicolour Dreamcoat*.

I buy two bags of Scillies' narcissus bulbs, Paper Whites, for Mum and for Hayley as a thank you present.

We don't see much on the journey home as there's low cloud all the way, but I sit next to Brett this time, so I don't care about what's outside the window.

Mum meets us at Penzance heliport and I say a reluctant goodbye to Brett's family. Hayley gives me a kiss and a hug, as does Brett's dad, and Brett sweeps a hand across my cricket cap, knocking it sideways. We do a high five. It's so romantic, I almost cry.

Oh yes, Alistair was on our helicopter too of course, wearing yet another colourful tie, and greets Mum rather enthusiastically. She looks pleased, if inappropriately dressed in a short skirt, and her face is over decorated, in my opinion.

Mum and I drive home in steady rain on the back road through Gulval, and on the sharp bend in the middle of the road is a male peacock, trailing its heavy tail on the wet tarmac. It's not a pheasant; it's definitely a peacock. It must live in one of the gardens here.

'Do you remember when you were little and you called them Poppycocks?'

'I didn't.'

'Yes you did, the first time you saw one you said "Look at the pretty poppycock".'

'Where did I get that word from?'

'Don't ask me, you've always been a strange child.'

I giggle at the idea of a peacock being a poppycock.

'I missed you,' she says.

'What did you do?' I ask.

'Well, believe it or not, I've started at a life class. I'm drawing again.'

Mum used to be a designer with a big design company in London before I was born. Afterwards there was no time for her to do anything except look after me, though she did the odd freelance job occasionally.

'And Arnold has finished the decorating.'

We drive through the little lanes, leaves flying off the low bent trees; it really feels like autumn. There's a school with children in the playground, skipping and playing games.

'Mum, when can I go back to school?'

'Oh Gussie, I don't think it's very wise to go back just yet. You have been quite ill, remember, and you'll only get a chest infection mixing with all those people and their colds, and you know what will happen if you do.'

'But Mum, I'm missing so much.'

'I know darling, I'm sorry. I have been thinking about it.'

There is a silence.

'How would you feel about a tutor coming to the house?'

'A tutor?' It sounds so nineteenth century, so archaic.

'Maybe.'

Mum says she had a disturbed but exciting night. She was woken at three by the sound of a growling cat. All our cats were inside pretending to be asleep. She was just in time to see a cat's ginger tail disappearing through the cat-flap. She grabbed it and it yowled and shot outside to where a large fluffy tabby waited and there was a great kafuffle and Mum managed to throw a kettle of cold water over them both before they ran off. She didn't go to sleep after that.

Charlie is ecstatic to see me, like a dog, not resentful at all; she lets me carry her around while I tell her how beautiful she is. (Cats really love the word 'beautiful'. They become hypnotised by the sound of the word.) Rambo hides under the table swishing his tail and Flo is out hunting.

I discover a pocket full of little yellow and red-brown periwinkle shells. I have carried home my found treasures, a memento of Paradise. I'll decorate my bower for my prospective mate. Perhaps I should learn how to sing too.

I give Mum her presents – the Paper Whites bulbs and a bar of chocolate that says on the label THANK YOU FOR LOOKING AFTER MY CAT that I bought in Tresco Abbey shop. I put the shells in a clear glass bowl with water in to bring the colour alive.

The young gull on the roof is still looking pissed off, so's his mum. He's like a lazy teenager who won't get off the sofa and go outside for exercise. A couch potato, grumpy, peevish, sulky. His dad has dark rings around his eyes – that's what it looks like, and his head is covered in brown-grey freckles. I think all adult herring gulls change their plumage slightly in the winter. His mouth turns down at the corners, which makes him look cross. Actually, they all look cross.

I tell Mum all about the lovely islands and how kind Hayley is and how it was okay sharing a room with her, and all about the rescued herring gull, and the boat rides and Tresco Abbey garden.

'Oh, if I'd known about the garden I might have come.'

'You'd love it, Mum.'

That night I think about the marvellous weekend and I feel so alive. Being alive is a bit like speed-reading. I have to experience everything, pack it in while there is still time.

The Poem for the Day today is 'The Embankment' (The Fantasia of a Fallen Gentleman on a Cold, Bitter Night) by TE Hulme.

> Once, in a finesse of fiddles found I ecstasy,
> In a flash of gold heels on the hard pavement.
> Now see I
> That warmth's the very stuff of poesy.
> Oh, God, make small
> The old star-eaten blanket of the sky,
> That I may fold it around me and in comfort lie.

I know exactly what he means. Being cold is the worst thing. My hands and feet go completely blue and numb if I get slightly chilled and I need a hot water bottle even in summer. 'He was killed in World War I, serving with the Royal Marine Artillery. He was expelled from St John's College, Cambridge, possibly for brawling (he is said to have carried a knuckle-duster around with him).' A poet with knuckle-dusters – strewth!

CHAPTER THIRTY

NOTE: MY NEW word for today is *eviscerate: to tear out the viscera or bowels of: to gut. n. evisceration – from viscera, the bowels.* That's an easy word for me to use straight away. It's exactly what I want to do to sss, eviscerate her, preferably through the hole in her navel.

Arnold is installing a bidet in the bathroom. Mum has a real thing about being clean and says a bidet is a necessity not a luxury. She says when you think about it most English people must walk around with less than clean bums. What a dreadful thought. Also, if you don't wash your bum before you get in the bath you are floating in your own filth. Yuk. And if you only have a shower how do you get at your privates or the underneath of your feet? It's different for boys of course. They are lucky, except for their feet.

I want to talk to Mum, but Arnold is having a cup of tea with her. I'll wait until he's gone.

'Has he gone?'

'Yes, why?'

'Oh nothing. What's for dinner?'

I can't face telling her what my research has come up with. Perhaps next time I'm in the car with her I'll say something. It's much easier to talk when I can't see her expressions. I can just imagine the shock on her face, the open mouth, the disbelief, the wide eyes. No, I'll wait for the right moment.

'Pasta and something easy with anchovies and olives. Tomatoes, we've got loads of tomatoes.'

'Goodie.' I flop on the sofa and go back to my book.

'Grate the cheese if you like.'

'When you say "if you like" do you really mean "if you

like" or do you mean…?'

'Just grate it, you precocious little beast.'

Later, before we cook the pasta, Arnold comes by with two ungutted mackerel for us.

'Caught twenty minutes ago,' he said. 'All right like that?'

'Oh, thank you Arnold. That's kind of you, yes I'll deal with them.' Mum sounds confident.

I look at them when he's gone. One is definitely dead, but the other one – I can still see life quivering in its tail part – rainbows and a flickering pulsing of blood. Oh God, is there still time to take it back to the sea? Can it still be alive twenty minutes after it was caught? That's awful.

'Mum! Mu-um! Come and see.'

I watch while she dispatches the poor fish by cutting off its head with a carving knife. It must be inherited. Her mother was ruthless with their chickens when it was time for them to go to the Free-Range Chicken Run in the Sky.

CHAPTER THIRTY-ONE

NOTE: WORD FOR the day: *Mullein – a tall, stiff, yellow-flowered woolly plant (Verbascum) of the Scrophulariaceae – popularly known as hag-taper, Adam's flannel, Aaron's rod, shepherd's club.*

I think I remember seeing those in the garden at Peregrine Point and on our little front path. They're flowering now. I'll impress Mum with my extensive floral knowledge.

(Does scrofulous come from the same route? Yes it does. The plants were thought to be a cure for Scrofula, or TB.)

It's raining and quite cold, but she's planting the bulbs. I hope they survive. Our garden is quite well sheltered and a suntrap when the sun shines. The blue hydrangeas have faded to muted pinks and mauves and remind me of Grandma's aprons.

I am making lists – I like making lists. Today's list is an alphabet of sayings. It's quite difficult.

A is for the Apple of my eye (Brett).

B is for his Beautiful mind. (I think that counts as metaphor because we can't actually see a mind, can we.)

C is for Clouds on my horizon (Mum's library books, my family research.)

D is for Dirty tricks – you know who goes in for those.

E is for Eat your heart out.

F is for False-faced. (Guess who.)

G is for Good Grief.

H is for Hang in there – meaning – don't give up.

I is for Ill-tempered – me at the moment.

J is for Jack of all trades – Arnold.

K is for Kettle of fish – a fine kettle of fish (my problems with library books).
L is for Light at the end of the tunnel (my transplant).
M is for Mother of all storms.
N is for No way!
O is for Odd man out – me.
P is for Panic attack.
Q is for Queue jumping.
R is for Ray of sunshine (what Grandpop called me).
S is for Safe as houses.
T is for Tearjerker – like *A Wonderful Life*.
U is for Upper crust.
V is for Vital spark.
W is for Walls have ears.
X is for X factor.
Y is for Young at heart – Mum
Z is for Zero in.

I do like rainy days. It's a wonderful excuse to mooch and read. I have just read RD Laing's *Conversations with Children*, which is all about his conversations with his own children:

Jutta [his wife] and I haven't been getting on very well recently. Natasha has become interested in glue and sellotape, in cutting things up and sticking them together.
    Just now she is dashing from one wall of my room to the other, thudding against them.
Ronnie: what are you doing?
Natasha: the heart.
Ronnie: the heart?
N: yes. (She continues thudding against the walls.)
R: and what does the heart do?

N: the heart loves (she stops dashing and thudding.)
R: the heart loves?
N: yes.
R: who? what?
N: the one heart loves many people.
R: the one heart loves many?
N: the one heart loves many many.

CHAPTER THIRTY-TWO

I THINK I may have done something rather stupid.

I haven't told Mum but I phoned Daddy to tell him about his grandfather being a famous photographer. He had no idea, he said, having cut himself off from his Cornish roots when he was young. He obviously did know about his father going to jail. That's why he and his mother left town, after all, and his parents eventually divorced. But he had no idea about his father's father. And thinking about it, it was his *father* who was the black sheep of the family, not Daddy. I phoned him when Mum was out shopping. He sounded pleased to hear my voice. I do love him so very much.

I wish he were here.

Sometimes you *do* get what you wish for.

I wish I could go to university, uni, I mean. Brett wants to go. I know it's a stupid thing to even think about. I probably won't even make secondary school at this rate.

If I had three wishes, no matter how impossible, they would be:

1. Mum and Daddy being happy together.
2. My heart being healthy.
3. Grandpop and Grandma being alive. All those wishes are useless so if by any chance a fairy asks me what I wish for, I better think up some more feasible requests:
1. Finding some live family.
2. Going to school.
3. A successful heart and lung transplant.

Bad night. My steam train heart wakes me... eyes sore so can't read for very long. Why are our problems so much worse in the dark? Anxieties well up when we're not able to keep watch, they break the dam and flood our dreams or wake us so we can worry in the drowning dark. Bad dreams when I did sleep: entire town flooded up to top of Barnoon Hill. We survived but everyone else dead.

Mum is in her bedroom window drawing what she sees from the window. She is concentrating hard, and looks happier than I have seen her for ages. I wish I could draw. It has never been my strong point. She now goes to the School of Painting twice a week.

'Mum...'

'Gussie, I'm working.'

'Can I talk to you, please? It's important.'

'Aren't you feeling well?"

'No, I'm fine. It's not that.'

'Later then, okay?'

I go back to my book and Rena Wooflie and Charlie.

Later is too late. I lose my nerve and say nothing.

I am going to be a writer. I've decided that's the only thing I can attempt to do without a decent education. My waste paper bin is already full of rubbish writing. Scribbled words lie strangled in twisted paper like squashed ants. I'm not going to get very far at this rate.

CHAPTER THIRTY-THREE

WE HAVE SEEN all the art in the Tate, St Ives, where I had a crab sandwich in the café on the top floor and Mum had a glass of wine, and now Mum and I are looking round the open artists' studios all over Down'long. This particular studio is rather dilapidated with rain coming in through the roof, but I think it adds to the character. There's a working pot-belly stove, with a long black pipe going out through the roof. A huge window looks out onto the rain-pitted beach, where a man throws a stick for a Jack Russell. (Do all Jack Russells suffer from Attention Deficit Hyperactive Syndrome?)

Maybe my Grandma had that. She never stopped talking, working, hurrying. And she was good at all sorts of things, which is part of the condition, apparently, so there are compensations.

Here are strange sculptures made of rusty metal and wood hung on the wooden walls and a large abstract painting in browns, greys and blacks on a huge easel. It smells of turpentine and oil paint and dust, new and old wood and raw canvas. Delicious.

There's a group of people talking to the artist – a square-shaped woman in a blue fisherman's smock and Doc Marten boots. I'd like some DMs.

I take a few photographs of the light patterns shed on the paint-splashed wooden floor, and the black stove and the old wooden plan chests that line one wall.

The next studio we visit is small and tidy and clean, with paintings of geometric paintings all on the theme of brown squares on black squares, so we don't stay long and I don't bother to record it on film. The next place we go to is where Mum has her lessons. I am very breathless going up the stairs to the entrance and there are impatient people behind us. I have to squat at the top and I'm in the way. Shit.

Shit shit shit.

Mum tells them, 'Sorry, my little girl's unwell, you'll have to wait a moment.'

My heart is racing, my head pounds, I'm faint and feel nauseous. When I have recovered my breath, someone finds me a chair and Mum phones for a taxi to take us home. Someone suggests an ambulance but Mum says no thanks, she'll be fine.

It is so old and beautiful in here, a wooden building with north facing windows, chairs and wooden easels stacked up in the corner, old oil paintings and recent drawings on the walls. Someone gets me water.

Home. I hate feeling ill when I'm not at home. Once I became ill when we were in Thailand and there was no doctor. We were moving that day to a house on a beach. Mum drove to there with me lying on the back seat looking very cyanosed, put me in bed under a ceiling fan, gave me Aspirin, cooled my pulse points with wet cloths and hoped I'd be okay.

And I was.

But when we saw my paediatric cardiologist in London, Mum told him what had happened and he said I shouldn't go to hot countries any more. Getting too hot or too cold would be a strain on my heart.

Daddy was hardly ever with us in the winter. He had to stay home and work. He did come to visit us once in Africa for three weeks. They shouted at each other.

Mum tucks me up on the sofa. I don't feel like climbing any more stairs just now. She has frown lines between her eyebrows as if she's angry with me for being ill, but I know she's only anxious, scared I'll die suddenly. What she doesn't seem to be aware of is that I could die of something else, not my failing heart, something totally unrelated to my pulmonary atresia. I could get run over by a bus – maybe not in St Ives, but when we're in Penzance or Truro. I could prick my finger on a rose and die of tetanus fever. I expect that's what the Sleeping Beauty had. Didn't she prick her finger and go into a coma?

Alistair has arrived. He examines me. He's gentle. I like him, even if he does look like a horse. A very *friendly* horse with an unusual taste in halters.

CHAPTER THIRTY-FOUR

WORD FOR YESTERDAY, but I have carried it over to today as I forgot to use it, was: *subterfuge: an evasive devise, especially in discussion; a refuge.*

Another reminder from the library arrived in the post today and I only just intercepted it in time. I'm not up to all this subterfuge. I feel especially guilty since Mum has suggested that Hayley tutors me at home. Brilliant idea. I do hope she agrees. I know she hasn't found a full time teaching job locally. Mum also wondered if I would like Brett's Dad, Steve, to teach me some Maths and Science. That would be so cool. I might even go to their house for lessons. That way I'd see more of Brett. Haven't seen him for a while.

Our young gull flies well now. He still comes back to roost on the roof at night with his parents. He must be feeding himself, as he no longer asks his parents for food. Or rather, he does ask sometimes, but his mum simply turns her head away and looks pointedly towards the harbour as if to say – dinner's out there, go and find it.

He is the same size and shape as his mother but is patterned like a tabby cat with brown speckles. He still can't talk properly though, and still has only one word to his vocabulary – Wheeee.

I haven't looked at the pond lately. It hasn't stopped raining for a week.

NOTE: The real word for today is: *Plash – a shallow pool, a dash of water, a splashing sound, to dabble in the water: to splash.*

I'll try and use it at least once today so I don't forget it.

Great news! Steve can give me one lesson a week, after school, and Hayley is coming twice a week to work with me on English. I don't think of that as work at all. I love books. Hayley's bringing me a reading list.

How ace is my mum!

I'm having a close look at the wedding photograph of Mum and Daddy in my room. She looks so pretty, so much younger than she looks now. After all, it was thirteen years ago. Age has suddenly caught up with her. Daddy is much younger than she is. She was a cradle snatcher, Grandma used to say.

Mummy says when you have been admired for your prettiness it's hard getting old. (One problem I won't have, then.) You feel the loss so much more than if you have never had that luck. She's says she's gone from hippie rock chick to Mother Theresa in a year.

Mother Theresa is a nun, isn't she? Does that mean Mum's not sleeping with Alistair? Or is she referring to the fact that she is dressing like a nun? She started to cover up her arms, neck, chest, legs, everything. What's left to expose? Shoulders, wrists and hands, and her feet. She still has pretty feet (apart from the hairy toes).

'Mum, are you sleeping with Alistair?'

'Gussie! My love life is my Own Private Business.'

'Yes, but are you, Mum? I think I have a right to know. Anyway, isn't it illegal for a doctor to be intimate with a patient?' I know that from a *Woman's Hour* programme.

'He's not my GP, he's yours.'

Ah. So that answers that question. She is sleeping with him.

I suppose she has every right to find someone else. Daddy left her for another woman even if the other woman has now left him. But somehow it makes me feel that my parents' divorce is one step closer. I know I hadn't really believed that my parents would get together again, but I can't face the idea that there isn't ever going to be that possibility: never to be a family again.

Here's what I know about my Cornish family:

My father is Jackson Stevens, born 1955.
His father was Hartley Stevens, born 1900, died 1975.
Hartley had a sister, Fay.
Daddy's mother was Molly Jackson, born 1920, died 1980.
Grandfather's father was a photographer, Amos Hartley Stevens.
That's it. Not much, but it's a start.

Having decided to become a writer, I have writer's block. Where shall I write? I haven't got a desk or anything in my room and I certainly don't want to write in the sitting room in full view of my mother. What if I want to write something rude or horrible about her? She'd see it. Also, I need a really good pen and a beautiful notebook. And what can I write about anyway? How do writers get to be writers? My journal is the only thing I write every day. I really would like a computer.

Perhaps photography would be easier. It's in my Cornish blood, after all. I hope I haven't lost that particular blood through my various operations. You do bleed a lot when you are undergoing major surgery. And I've had lots of other people's blood in transfusions. I feel as if I have got some Cornishness deep inside me, nevertheless. I feel as if this is Home with a capital H.

We have breakfast out, Mum and me, every Saturday. We take turns choosing where to go. Today we are in a café on Tregenna Hill and sit by a window so we can see people passing. Claire is joining us with Gabriel. Mum is having the Full English. She says she deserves it after a week of All

Bran and apricots. I'm having a bacon sarni. That sounds as if it could be Strine. I'll ask Brett. There are lots of shoppers in the street and people stop and talk to each other. I expect everyone knows everyone else. It must make you feel safe when you recognise most people around you. It's like a huge clan or one large extended family.

At the next table there is a family with a little girl about four. She's wearing a pink dress and eating a huge pink ice-cream. She says to her daddy, 'I'm going to cut off your head and eat your brains with a spoon.' He looks mock horrified and she screams with laughter.

There's a small group of elderly men standing on the corner at the bottom of the hill by the bank. There's no seat, but they gather there in a row on the narrow pavement most days and watch the world go by, laughing and greeting old friends, and I suppose talking about their aches and pains, and who has just died, and how the local rugby teams are doing. One of them I recognise from the fishermen's lodges but he doesn't notice me.

Claire invites us out to their place tomorrow for lunch. We'll meet the rest of the family, unless the surf is good somewhere, in which case Phaedra and Troy will follow the waves. Gabriel is of course up in his tree. He has built a veritable palace of platforms and ropes. All the trees have lost their leaves and only the bare bones are visible. The chicks are now pullets and the kittens have all gone to new homes. The floppy-eared rabbits haven't changed a bit, except that they spend more time in their hutch. The ducks are still waddling or limping and worrying the grass.

I have a present for Gabriel: a Darth Vader sword. Last time we came here he was playing at Star Wars with a rolled paper weapon. Mum said not to give it to him until we leave for home but it starts to rain very heavily and Gabriel comes in looking bedraggled and miserable so I give him the gift. He unwraps it and his little face lights up. He loves it. Claire isn't too happy though. And Phaedra and Troy, who have been in their rooms, come out to see what the horrible noise is, and Troy, who is about six feet tall, confiscates the offending toy that's flashing lights and playing a dreadful tinny sound, and puts it on a high shelf, and Gabriel goes back outside in a huff.

'He'll be all right, dear of him,' Claire smiles at me.

Phaedra is auburn-haired, slender and straight-backed and looks like a ballet dancer. Troy looks like a surfer – blond straggly hair and tanned still from a summer of riding waves. He's taller than his sister.

'Sorry, that was my fault,' I say.

Troy goes back to his room and his music and Phaedra, who is the most beautiful girl I have ever seen, joins us at the huge kitchen table, which their father built. He comes in soaking wet and dries his hair on a towel. He washes his hands and sits down at the head of the table in a string-seated hand crafted chair with arms.

'How's your back?' he asks Mum.

'Better thanks, much better, thanks to Claire.'

'And what are you up to, young Gussie?'

'I've been taking photographs of old men,' I say. I have my camera with me.

'What old men?' Mum is disbelieving.

'Old fishermen, mostly, on the harbour.'

'My mother's father was a good photographer, wasn't he, Claire?'

'He was, honey, yes.'

That's the trouble with modern cameras. If you own a camera and can take a picture that's in focus you think you are a good photographer.

'Moss, your Mum's arrived.'

A tall, handsome woman with a halo of frizzy white hair

appears from under a large black umbrella, which she shakes vigorously at the doorway before taking off her wellington boots.

'Hello, everyone.'

'It's very plashy out today, isn't it,' I say, to impress them with my vocabulary.

They look at each other as if I'm mad.

We're all having tea – Mum made a carrot cake especially, and I helped. They provide most of the food though: duck-egg Spanish omelette with courgettes and herbs from the garden and home-made bread, cooked that morning by Gabriel's dad. Gabriel comes in shortly after his gran and sits next to her, stuffing himself with everything in sight and gazing longingly at his sword on the high shelf. She puts an arm around him to hug him and he wriggles out of her embrace.

Phaedra goes to sixth-form college by bus every day and Troy is in his last year at St Ives School. He says it's pretty boring. Can't be half as boring as being at home all the time, I think, but don't say.

After tea we play Monopoly. Or rather I play Monopoly with Gabriel and Phaedra and their gran. We play at the big table. I sit on a very handsome chair, which has pale coloured wood arms and a string seat. The other dining chairs are different shapes but all hand-made, or craftsman-built.

Treasure is asleep on a blue and yellow rag rug by the Rayburn, enjoying a well-earned holiday after bringing up her babies. She doesn't seem at all bothered at not having them around any more. She's got Spider of course, her best friend Spider. He is curled up on a beautiful chair, like no other chair I have ever seen. It has curved arms and a seat of woven string and the back looks as if it has been carved from one piece of wood. There are similar stools, I notice.

'Did your dad make the chair?' I ask Phaedra.

'No, Grandpa Darling did. He made furniture too.'

There's the lovely homely smell of clothes airing above the Rayburn, almost scorching but not quite.

Phaedra is in a St Ives Youth Theatre production soon. It's a local theatre company for 6–18 year-olds, and she has been going to it for years. They do all sorts of musicals, like *The Wizard of Oz* and *Joseph and the Amazing Technicolour Dreamcoat* and they did *Fame* in the summer. She has to go to rehearsals several times a week in an old Wesleyan chapel in St Ives that has been made into a theatre. She's got long rubbery legs and this amazing fuzzy hair the colour of sunsets.

Gabriel is very quiet. Does he still speak? I don't think I have heard him say a word today. It's stopped raining and he wants to go outside with his sword. He speaks!

'Is that all right, love? (to Claire). 'Go on then, Monkey,' says his gran, and he whoops for joy and climbs like a chimp to the high shelf.

'He's got a crush on you, Gussie.' Phaedra says.

'Really? A crush on me?'

'Yeah, he thinks you're geet ace.'

'What does that mean?'

'It's Cornish slang for wonderful,' says their gran.

The game sort of falls apart when he goes, which is a shame as I had managed to buy two of the orange properties, Park Lane and three stations. Phaedra says she has homework to do and goes to her room. Mum and the other adults are drinking wine and laughing. Mum looks quite young when she laughs.

I'd like to stay here forever.

When their gran says she better get back to her cabin, I say, 'Oh, please may I have a look inside?'

'Gussie! Gabriel's grandmother doesn't want to be bothered with you, do you?'

'She's very welcome. She can meet Five-toes.'

I put on my parka and wellies and we set off for the cabin along the muddy path. The ducks are happily shovelling grass and looking for worms I suppose. Gabriel's dad follows us out in order to put the creatures back in their hutches for the night.

A deep voice – for an eight year old – comes from the crown of the palace-tree: 'May the force be with you.'

We giggle.

Gabriel's gran holds the brolly over me and tells me to go in. The cabin is just as cosy on the inside as it looked from the outside. Like a gypsy caravan but more modern. The stove is on and I warm my hands at it – they've gone numb. The large fluffy cat that I last saw on the bridge over the stream is curled up on the sofa next to the stove.

'Have I the pleasure of meeting Five-toes?' I stroke her head gently and she opens one eye and glares at me.

I confess that I peered in the window last time I was here but Gabriel's gran doesn't seem to mind. I don't know what to call her. I have forgotten her name if anyone ever told me. Old people do seem to give up their identity when they become mothers or fathers or grandparents. They just become someone's gran, a nameless unidentified being, anonymous. It must be awful.

Even the cat has a name.

A rather lovely oil painting of a Cornish beach hangs on one wall. I study it.

'One of mine,' says Gabriel's gran. Wow, she must have been to art school.

The photograph I saw through the window is of course a portrait of her when she was young. It could be Phaedra, except that the hairstyle and dress are old-fashioned. There's a signature, which I cannot read as I haven't got my reading glasses.

'Is it you?'

'Yes, my love, it is me. When I was about Phaedra's age. We're alike aren't we? I had that same colour hair.'

She smiles a wide, soft-lipped smile, as if she is suddenly that girl again. That happens when my Mum smiles. She can be looking so sad and fed up and old and if I make her smile her face lights up and youth floods back into her face. Then she becomes herself again – Lara Stevens – not just Mum.

'Who took the photograph? It looks very professional.'

'Very perceptive of you. My father: he was a good photographer.'

'May I take a photograph of you, now?'

'Me, now? Oh I don't think so. I'm too old to have my photograph taken.'

'How about with Gabriel?'

'Take one of Gabriel on his own.

'I've been taking photographs of the men in the fishermen's lodges. It would be good to have some of local women too.'

'I'll think about it dear.'

I take a photograph of Five-toes instead, which is probably out of focus. I need varifocals.

My Grandma used to tell me about the time when she and I were locked in a lavatory in the basement of a little gallery that was about to close for the weekend. The knob had fallen off the locking mechanism and fallen on a floor littered with boxes. I was about two. She hadn't got her glasses on and couldn't see where the knob had rolled. She asked me to be her eyes while she sung 'Two Old Ladies Locked in the Lavatory'. I found it, luckily, or we'd be there still. What would she have done if we had been locked there from Monday to Saturday, nobody knew they were there. We could have survived on water from the washbasin and we could have chewed bits of cardboard box to stave off hunger. I expect she had some extra strong peppermints in her coat pocket: she usually did.

We drive back along the road through Halsetown – no horses on the road today, they are all munching happily in their field – and take a short cut down a very small lane where we come across a dear little dog wandering along looking lost – you know the way on-the-loose dogs run sideways and have a mad look in their eyes. He has a collar on and we grab him. No name or address. Mum wraps him in an old mac because he's rather muddy and I hold him on my lap while she drives along the lane until we come to a drive. We go up the drive to a big house, but there's no one in. We try the next cottage but there's no one there either. He's so sweet, just a black mongrel, his big dark eyes peering out from long straggly hair. He sits very quietly curled up on my lap. I think he must be tired and hungry.

'No We Can't Keep Him,' says Mum.

'Did I say a word?' I am incredulous that she can read my mind. That's awful.

'You don't need to. We'll take him to the vet, he might be micro-chipped.'

Our vet checks for a chip but there isn't one. The puppy is a bitch about twelve weeks old.

'I expect she escaped from a garden,' he says. 'We'll look after her, until we can find her owners.'

'She's got fleas,' I say, 'I killed one in the car.'

'Oh, great,' says Mum, 'now I'll have to wash the mac.'

'You'd have to anyway, it's all muddy.'

In the car I tell Mum about a story Gabriel's gran told me. She said that Gabriel thought Poppy Day was Puppy Day and he was going to get a puppy. He was really disappointed.

Mum reminds me of when I was little and pretended to be a police puppy, whatever that is. I remember thinking myself into the mind of a little dog and I spent hours on all fours yapping and panting and insisting she put on my lead and take me for walks. It drove her potty.

CHAPTER THIRTY-FIVE

NOTE: WASPS FEED their young on insects that are injurious to crops.

I always thought that they were of no use to anyone or anything, but I read that in a book called *Out with Romany Once More* by Bramwell Evens. I bought it for 50p at a local fleamarket where Mum bought two jars of home-made marmalade and an Edwardian postcard from Southend-on-Sea. Romany lives in a vardo, whatever that might be. I can't find it in my *Chambers Dictionary*. It must be a gypsy caravan or cabin or something. He's a countryman who teaches a farmer's son called Tim about wildlife. I bought it because of the lovely monochrome illustrations of animals. There's a nameplate – PRESENTED TO LAURENCE LOCKWOOD, FIRST PRIZE CLASS 3 (JUNIOR), UPTON CROSS CP SCHOOL, and it must have been about 1950, because the book was published in 1940, then reprinted in 1941, 42, 43, 44, and 1949. So it must have been really popular. Romany had a programme on radio, but Mum doesn't remember it.

Tim often spends a night in the vardo with Romany so they can go out in the early hours to see badgers. Can you imagine a child being allowed to do that today? Stay in a strange man's home all night? I don't think so.

I've just made a list of all the creatures we helped to support when we were renting Peregrine Cottage:

1. Slugs – a purple giant came in under the front door at night to eat any leftover cat food in the porch.
2. Spiders – ate flies.
3. Cat fleas – ate cats.

4. Woodlice – ate wood.

5. Fruit flies – liked rotting fruit but went really mad for Mum's whisky.

6. Bees – ate nectar from garden flowers.

7. Butterflies – ditto.

8. Slow-worms – what do they eat? I think there was a huge colony of them under the floorboards of the porch.

9. Crickets – haven't faintest idea what their food is, but we had loads of them.

10. Harvest Mice and Voles – crumbs.

11. Small Birds – sunflower seeds and peanuts etc that we put out specially, and leftover rice and bread.

12. Three Cats – cheese, fish, Greek yoghurt, curried chicken and cat food.

13. Stray cats – crept in at night to steal cat food.

14. Badgers – unsalted peanuts and all leftovers except green veg.

15. Pop the herring gull, who ate everything except rice and veg. He ate chips though. Poor Pop, I wonder if he survived. He swallowed a fishing hook.

I've also made a list of some of the things we have in our home that someone else has owned before – recycled furniture, car boot finds, not counting the objects that belonged to Grandma and Grandpop:

1. A low wooden stool carved with a blackbird on the bough of an oak tree.

2. Lace linen tablecloths, lots of them, a whole cupboard full. I don't know why Mum buys them, because we never use them, except perhaps at Christmas. Maybe she buys them because Grandma was always lace-making and embroidering and Mum never appreciated

the handiwork when she was a child.

4. Many odd cups and saucers, antique mugs and plates of very pretty blues and pinks with roses.

5. Bowls of all sizes, mixing bowls, pudding bowls, pretty bowls for sweets.

6. Forty-six coloured glasses and glass jugs. Anyone would think we have home-made lemonade or cocktail parties or something. Mum does have a special glass for whisky – well, several special glasses, one green cut glass that cost a lot of money and has a narrow base so it often gets knocked over; one opaque white tumbler and one plain glass tumbler with a pattern of coloured circles. I usually drink my sparkling water from the bottle, which really pisses her off. She says I'll Never be a Lady.

7. Our dining table comes from a junk shop but it's a 1950s Ercol Plank table and we have various Ercol chairs – the ones with the stick backs, from car boot sales. We have two 1930s Lloyd Loom armchairs, painted white and with seats covered in deckchair canvas striped orange and white and blue. I do wish she'd kept Grandpop's rocker. She could have reupholstered it in that striped canvas.

8. Some of Mum's best cooking pots are from car boot sales – Le Creuset cast iron enamelled in orange. She says they are dreadfully expensive to buy them new and she got them For a Song.

9. She has about ten old enamel colanders. My favourite is a dark blue one that used to be Grandma's. I can still see her in her tiny kitchen, her round red arms fighting with a rabbit's insides, steam shooting out of the pressure cooker with a piercing whistle. I don't remember her actually using the colander, which is probably why her cabbage was always soggy.

10. We even get some of our bed linen from car boot sales, real linen, or pink or blue striped cotton sheets and frilly edged pillow cases with embroidery on.
They feel so cool against the skin.
11. Our lampshades are glass bowls from the thirties. They have splodges of colour on them and the light makes the colours come alive.
12. Old linen and lace cloths that Mum makes into curtains, and old table napkins. (Mum hates paper serviettes and always packs a linen napkin to take on long journeys or holidays. She says it keeps her feeling civilised in the most uncomfortable situations – when I'm in hospital, or when we are stuck on a broken down train.) It's like her comfort blanket.

I think I'll concentrate on collecting old books on birds and nature. There were so many interesting ones at the cottage on the cliff and I learned so much from them and loved the language of them, the old fashioned tales of close encounters with wildlife.

I recently found a *Filmgoer's Annual* from the fifties. I'm keeping it to send to Daddy on his birthday. He'll be forty-six in November. I wonder what Mum is getting him? But I suppose now she Despises and Loathes him she won't get him anything.

This will be our second Christmas without Daddy, or Grandma, or Grandpop.

It will be dreadful. And look what I have become since Daddy left us, and my grandparents died: *a liar. A sneaky sly thief and a liar. A deceiver, misleader, beguiler, bamboozler, a phoney, a wolf in sheep's clothing, an ass in lion's skin, a jackdaw in peacock's feathers. A fibber, fabricator, fabulist, falsifier, a mythomaniac, a snake in the grass.*

CHAPTER THIRTY-SIX

I DREAMT THAT we were driving along, Daddy and Mum and me, and two little birds, blue-tits or sparrows, who were dancing together in the air, twittering loudly, flew into the windscreen of our car and were smashed to pieces. I woke with feelings of dread and guilt and sadness in the middle of the night to an awful sound, a sound like a blackbird being slowly crushed in the jaws of a cat. Then a low hoo-hoo of an owl. I think maybe the squeal could have been a screech owl, not an injured blackbird. I looked out the window onto a clear starry sky, the orange yellow planet of Mars right above the house.

NOTE: I looked up *vardo* in Mum's *Concise Oxford Dictionary* (it's huge and you can't read the words without a magnifier). It means wagon. Word for the day: *prosaic, like prose; unpoetical; matter-of-fact; common-place; dull.*

Mrs Lorn is whistling away while she's changing the bed sheets. I don't recognise the hymn. Mum is at her Life Class, which sounds like they should be teaching her how to live not how to draw. I don't know why she wants to do it anyway, because she knows how to draw already, but she says she is out of practice and you must keep on doing something to remain good at it.

'Mrs Lorn?'

'Yes dear?'

'Do you still work at Peregrine Point?'

'Yes, I do, my 'ansome.' She is now whistling 'All Things Bright and Beautiful', I think it's supposed to be, which brings back my guilt. They sang it at the funeral I went to.

'Is the owner back now or is someone else renting it?'

'The owner is back, dear, yes.'

'Is he famous, Mrs Lorn?'

'He's a very nice gentleman, dear.'

I knew it, I was right, it's a man. But what does he do?

'What does he do, Mrs Lorn, for a living?'

'He's retired my love, I suppose, he don't do any work as far I can see.'

'Oh, you don't know what it was he did when he worked?'

'No dear, I don't pry into other people's business. I do his cleaning and he pays me, that's all I know.'

'Mrs Lorn?'

'Gussie dear, what is it?' She is struggling with the hoover hose, which has a mind of its own and won't be tamed.

'Is there a gull still on the roof at Peregrine Point?'

'Gull? Gulls are everywhere, gulls are, my cheel'. Can't get away from them.'

It's quite cold and the sea looks wintry and dangerous as if it bears a terrible grudge and has a temper only just under control.

I spend the day indoors reading and trying to write poems, feeling strangely sad and melancholy and looking out of the windows of my room. It's easier to write poetry in this mood. Writing about happiness is much harder.

On days like today when everything seems like shit in my life, the day stares in at me with its sparkling sea and salty air, and shouts – look at me, aren't I beautiful?

Late on, the sun appears only to be immediately swallowed by the sea, and lives on shining upwards through the sticky surface. It reminds me of something that Bridget said: 'Silver is a secret, white is sorrow, green is a forest that takes sorrow away, and gold is a glimmer of hope.' That child is a natural poet. I just don't think in that way. I am prosaic – Ha! I've used my word of the day. The Poem of the Day is 'The Heavenly City' by Stevie Smith. The note at the bottom of the page is a quote from Stevie Smith: 'I can't make up my mind if God is good, impotent or unkind.'

If there is a God, an invisible to us, omnipotent power, what are we supposed to be *for*? Why were we created? What's the reason for life? Are we here on Earth for a purpose? More than simply carrying on our genes? Perhaps we are here to record the wonders of creation: a field of daisies, a lion's roar, a butterfly wing, the scent of apples. But at the same time we'd have to mention the horrors of life on Earth – we can't ignore earthquakes that kills thousands, floods and mud slides that bury whole towns, hurricanes, volcanoes, drought that kills painfully slowly. We might as well be tiny insects in a termite hill, God an elephant stomping on us.

Mum and I have more or less stopped listening to news programmes on the radio or on telly. It's too depressing. We heard that a little boy who has recently had a heart and lung transplant has died. It's strange how sad we feel. We didn't know him. But we had been following his progress.

When did I first know about death? As a thing that happens to us all? I think it was when I was about ten and I saw a programme about the Second World War. A bulldozer shovelling naked corpses into a heap. I'll never forget it. My brain couldn't take it in straight away. They looked like a tangled pile of Pick-Up Sticks. I felt physically sick. And when I asked Grandma if she and Grandpop were going to die she said of course not, she had no intention of dying.

But she was wrong. She was wrong.

Or it could have been when I was really quite small and in hospital. A five-year-old in the next bed – he had no hair – died in the night and I heard his mother and father sobbing behind the curtain.

And somehow I became aware that I would in all likelihood die before I reach adulthood, like children in third world countries who die of measles and AIDS and TB.

But as Grandpop said about Grandma's meagre harvest of courgettes – 'Never mind the quantity, taste the quality.'

I truly believe that if the world around you is beautiful then you will feel that life is worth living, but if you are surrounded by ugliness it is hard to be contented. Looking out the window at the town's higgledy skyline, the orange roofs, the little streets and hills of St Ives, the breathing bay beyond, with the grey cloak of the sky, I am glad to be alive, glad of soaring gulls, glad of the scent of salt air, the reassuring whoosh of waves, glad of my cats' arching backs and curling tails, glad my heart is still beating.

Mum is in a bad way. If it's not her back it's her hormones. She's getting hot flushes and she is bleeding heavily between periods. I would have thought she was too old for periods but apparently not. She's gone to see her doctor – not Alistair. I'm mooching with the cats. It's murky and cold and I don't want to go out. I see in the local paper there's a place called Arts and Artists in town and they have books about local artists and potters and writers. Maybe I can find out more about great-grandfather Amos Hartley Stevens. Not today though. Unless I phone.

'Hello, this is Augusta Stevens. I wonder if you have any books about a man called Amos Hartley Stevens, my great-grandfather, actually. Oh, yes I could come round. What about tomorrow? Oh, okay, next week, yes, thanks, thank you, I'll see you then.'

Strewth, it's so easy, doing research. Perhaps I'll be a historian.

Mum phones the vet and he tells her the puppy has found a good home.

CHAPTER THIRTY-SEVEN

I'VE DUG OUT a few of Mum's antique clothes – lace and silk petticoats and flimsy muslin dresses that she wore when she was young (she was into old things even then as she was a hippie) and she's too fond of them to throw them away, and I'm hanging them up by windows and taking photographs of them. With a window open and morning light flowing through them they look alive, or as if ghosts are wearing them.

There's a creamy Japanese embroidered jacket with flared sleeves, a large bird of paradise embroidered on the front, and flowers and gold threads running through the blues and pinks and beiges. I wonder who it was made for originally. Did an empress wear it? Or a geisha?

That's the charm of old clothes and furniture and china, the fact that they have a past, a history, mysterious and unknown. We have all these ghosts surrounding us, with us every day.

I like to think that Grandpop and Grandma are keeping watch over us. Mum especially at the moment. She needs looking after: a good enough reason for me to find my Cornish family here. Okay, they aren't actually her family, only by marriage, but they would be better than nothing. She'll be alone in the world one day and it makes me unhappy to think of her with no one to care for her. Who knows where Alistair will be? He might go off her, like Daddy did and find a younger woman. Why does she choose younger men all the time – well, twice? Why can't she find a man her own age? I suppose they're already married, or if they're divorced there must be something wrong with them, or they're gay.

I hope Alistair will be around to comfort her when I die.

I dream about a bird of paradise and other exotic birds coming in my window and playing games, hunting treasure buried under the duvet. They are all brightly coloured and highly intelligent. A lyrebird struts and displays. The bird of paradise walks right up to my face as I lie in bed and lets me stroke his yellow head and push my fingers deep into his chest feathers so I feel his flesh. He looks me in the eye and touches his black beak to my lips. I wake with the strange feeling of the packed quills against my fingertips.

CHAPTER THIRTY-EIGHT

HAYLEY IS HERE with loads of her books and we have had a fantastic morning talking about poetry and novels. She loves books and knows many poems by heart. She and I each choose a poem and talk about it. She chooses a poem by an American called Raymond Carver. He died aged fifty after cancer. He was an alcoholic for many years before he met his second wife, ten years before he died. And he was very aware of his own mortality. Hayley says he wrote some of his best work in his last years. He wrote short stories too and always made them out of his own experiences, writing about fishing and being drunk and rows with his family. In his poem 'Cherish' he talks about his wife gathering roses given for their late wedding. He calls her 'wife' while he can, because he knows he hasn't long to live.

I wish I could make something as beautiful as his poem before I die.

I choose Sharon Olds' poem 'I Go back to May 1937', one of Ruth Padel's choice of Sunday Poems in the *Independent* newspaper. It's all about a photograph of Sharon Olds' parents before they were married and before she was born. The poet says she wants to go to them and say 'don't marry each other. You are going to make yourselves very unhappy.' But she doesn't because she wants to have been born. She wants to live.

Yes, I go along with that; I want to live, I... I... I...

CHAPTER THIRTY-NINE

ARTS AND ARTISTS has shelves of specialist books on local art and artists and a small gallery area for exhibitions of paintings. The man has heard of my great-grandfather, and looks him up on the internet. Ohmygod, it's wonderful. I want a computer.

Amos Hartley Stevens, born in St Ives, 1880. Studied at Plymouth 1896; Royal College of Art 1899. Married Mary Menzies of London in 1900. Returned to St Ives 1893. AHS was a *plein air* painter for a while, combined painting with photography; opened a photographic studio on Tregenna Place. They had four children: Hartley, Menzies, John and Fay. So, my grandfather Hartley Stevens had three siblings. I wonder what happened to them?

There's no record of their lives at Arts and Artists. There are some marvellous books here though, and I take the opportunity to look at some.

Bernard Leach the potter lived here. His pots look rather stodgy to me, brown and dark and treacly. But they fetch loads of money in auctions. Mum told me that. She thought she had found a large plate of his at a car boot sale, but it wasn't his or any of his students, and she didn't like it so she gave it to the cats. They appreciate the gravy coloured glaze, licking it clean every day. She has learnt her lesson and now only buys things she really likes and can live with.

I like the paintings of John Anthony Park. *Morning Tide*, one of the books here, is about his life. He was born in 1878 and died 1962. He painted landscapes and seascapes and actually lived for a while at 3 Bowling Green, that's next door but one to where we live. That was in 1923. How exciting, a famous painter in our terrace. I wonder why there isn't a blue plaque on the wall? Where we lived in London there were blue plaques all over the place, as so many famous people have lived in Camden.

Oh, what's this? A large book with a photograph of a chair on the front cover, and it looks very like one of the beautiful chairs at the Darlings' house.

'I have to close now, my dear,' says the man. 'I'm sorry to have to throw you out, but we are setting up a new exhibition. Have you found what you are looking for?'

'I would like to come back and do some more research please.'

'We're open again next Thursday, 11–4.'

'I'll be back.'

CHAPTER FORTY

THE WORD OF the day is *entrepreneur: one who undertakes an enterprise esp. a commercial one, often at personal financial risk.*

I have been cutting out Ruth Padel's columns. She explains the quality of modern poems, internal rhymes as opposed to end of line rhymes, half rhymes that echo through the work. She makes poetry so much more interesting and accessible. I hope there will be a book of the collected articles.

It's Hallowe'en. There have been huge pumpkins for sale in the shops. Mum doesn't believe in Hallowe'en, but when three small children appear at the back door in witch and wizard costumes, their Mum lurking in the background, and ask 'Trick or treat?' she gives them apples from our tree. They don't look terribly grateful for the 'treat', but Mum shuts the door before they can play a trick on us.

There will be a firework display on the harbour beach on Guy Fawkes' Day and she says we can go to it if the weather is okay. If not, we can watch from my window. The cats hate fireworks and I might have to stay and comfort them instead of going to the beach. One year in London I made a terrific guy, with Mum's help, and sat at the corner of our street collecting money. It was a great success, and I raised five pounds in two days.

I think I'd be a good entrepreneur.

I have posted Daddy's birthday present and card. I wonder what he will be doing on his birthday? Sometimes we used to go out to have dinner together in a Greek café in Camden Town. It was his favourite place to eat because they knew him there and made a big fuss of him. He had used the café as a location in a short film he'd made. It never got shown though. But they treated him as if he was a famous film director, and naturally he liked that. Maybe he'll go there on his own? Poor Daddy, he must be so lonely without us.

I phone him and wish him Happy Birthday. He loves the *Filmgoer's Annual*, and the card. He's off to a party with someone called Luk, a girl from Thailand. She's nineteen. Why did he have to tell me her age? I don't care who he's taking out or how old she is. I certainly won't tell Mum. He acts like having a young girl friend is some kind of trophy he's won for being Mr Wonderful. And he isn't, is he? He's left us, he hasn't kept his marriage promises and he's a stupid vain waste of space.

Bonfire Day is a washout. I hope the weather will be good for the New Year's Eve celebrations. St Ives is The Place to be at New Year.

The long tube hose of the carpet cleaner won't slide up and down without falling out, and Mrs Lorn can't find the missing part. Mum and I are going to Penzance to get it mended and do some shopping. It's pouring with rain, foggy, and the roads are flooded.

When we get out of the car in the car park Mum removes the hose out the boot and wraps it around her. I hold the brolly. The hose comes off her shoulders and wriggles onto the ground like an unruly python, and she drags it behind her to the shop. We are laughing hysterically. The man says he can't mend it without the missing part, but he agrees to replace the hose. But he doesn't want the hose taking up room in his workshop, so we have to go through the whole ridiculous procedure again – out into the monsoon rain with the python trying to escape and back to the car. We are so wet we can't face shopping so we drive home slowly, on the back road, keeping to the middle of the road where there is less water. Mum's fun to be with sometimes. No peacocks today.

I remind her of when we were in Thailand one winter, driving through terrible weather, after a scary boat trip in thunder and lightning; the road had totally disappeared under water, and it was much more difficult to stay on the track. There were no windscreen wipers, and one of our carload of children had to lean out the front passenger window and wipe the screen with her hand so Mum could see where she was going. We were up to the axle, but we got through. The water buffaloes looked happy.

I often think of the times we spent in hot countries each winter. I used to chase hedgehogs around the outside of the house in the dark – that was in Africa – and in Thailand I had several American friends who lived in the same compound as us. We had night-time barbecues, toasting marshmallows over the fire.

I'm sending a Christmas card to Sergeant Ginnie Witherspoon, the wildlife warden I met, and to Mr Writer. I do love Christmas.

Over every shop in Fore Street men have fixed real Christmas trees. They all have white lights on them (the trees not the men) and after dark the town is lit up like a fairy tale. From my window I can see more fairy lights swaying in the wind on Smeaton's Pier.

Bridget and her Mum have invited me to go with them to the parish church on Christmas Eve for the early evening service, which is especially for children. I hope Siobhan won't be there. No, of course she won't.

I'm not sure I have the guts to go in the church again. Are liars allowed? If we were Catholics, I could confess my sins and be forgiven, but we're not.

We have covered our little cherry tree in the front garden in lights.

Father Christmas will appear at a local fête. Obviously I no longer believe in Father Christmas, but I can pretend, for appearances' sake – that's pretending, not lying, there's a huge difference. And I hope to buy some presents there. I wonder if Gabriel believes, and Bridget?

The big question is what to get Daddy. I got him nail clippers last year, which he really appreciated, but unfortunately they are still working so I can't get him any more.

Why are men so difficult to buy presents for? Women and girls are easy. We like pretty things, usually, things we wouldn't buy for ourselves, like bracelets and necklaces and hair slides and t-shirts and cuddly toys. I, of course would prefer book tokens to any of those, but I know Mum likes to get perfume and clothes and glittery stuff.

Grandma always wanted silk scarves. She had loads of them. Never wore them as far as I remember, just kept them in a drawer and let me play with them. I would unfold them carefully from their tissue paper, wrap them around my waist or head and pretend to be a pirate or a highwayman, or if the scarf pattern was tiger skin or a leopard or zebra, I would be Tarzan.

Dad had a thing about old Tarzan films. So did I. I would leap from chair to chair and table to stool at Grandma's shouting 'Aah Eeh Aah!'

As Grandma used to say, 'Those were the days,' as if anything that happened a long time ago was necessarily better than what was happening in the present.

'Mum.'

'Yes?' She puts down her magazine and peers at me over her glasses, which she only wears at home, as she hates herself in them. She keeps one pair in the bathroom, one in the kitchen, and one in the bedroom for reading in bed and one in her bag. That's the theory anyway. In practice the cases are in place but the glasses could be anywhere at all: under piles of magazines, in with the laundry, in the garden. One day we were out together and she couldn't find her car keys in her bag, so she emptied it and out came nine pairs of specs – nine! Several were old spares that didn't really work any more and that she said she was going to take to be recycled at the opticians.

'What is it, Gussie, stop staring at me as if I'm a Martian.'

'Sorry. Mum did you know your grandparents?'

'On your Grandpop's side I did. His father was also in the Royal Navy. He was awarded the *Croix de Guerre* at Gallipoli.'

'The what?'

'The *Croix de Guerre*. It's the highest award given by the French to a foreign national.'

'How did he win it?'

'Well, he was a signalman on a ship carrying two French admirals. They were off the coast of Turkey and my grandfather, up in the crow's nest, was signalling the enemy's position to the allied ships. He was shot by a sniper from the shore and the bullet embedded itself in his forehead. He carried on signalling for two hours before he collapsed from loss of blood.'

'Wow! Did he die?'

'No. It was a spent bullet, it had travelled a long way before it hit him and hadn't got the force of a fresh one.'

'Oh.'

'Yes, and he was awarded the medal there and then by the French admirals. He was transferred straight away to a hospital ship but the enemy torpedoed that and sunk it, and he lost the medal. He survived to tell the tale though, but he only told my Pop, his son, a little while before he died. He'd never mentioned his war before that. My Pop got in touch with the French Admiralty and they issued my Grandad with a replacement *Croix de Guerre* three weeks before he died.'

'Have you got the medal?'

'Yes, I'll find it for you to see.'

'So my great-grandfather was a hero?'

'Yes, Guss, a real hero.'

'What was his name?'

'Alfred William.'

I will take a photograph of the medal as part of my family history.

So, I have two famous ancestors that I know of. Now would have been a good moment to tell Mum about my research, but the phone rings and she is billing and cooing to Alistair.

CHAPTER FORTY-ONE

THE CHRISTMAS FETE or 'Fair Mo' is in the town hall, which has been specially decorated with balloons and fake holly wreaths. It still smells of that silvery white talcum sort of dust you put on the wooden floor of a dance hall. (There was a dance here a few days ago.) I have a month's pocket money to spend.

Outside, next to a sculpture by Barbara Hepworth, the Youth Band is playing carols. Inside, stalls sell hand-made greetings cards and present tags, silver and gold fir cones, bowls of hyacinth bulbs and other Christmassy plants, home-made jams and pickled onions and tomatoes with lids of scalloped holly-patterned fabric. One stall sells raffle tickets and the prizes are on show. Mum buys four for a pound in the hope of winning a bottle of whisky.

There's a Santa Claus downstairs in the 'Grotto' and a queue of expectant little children on the stairs. Nearly all the voices at the fair are local, high-pitched and loud with excitement.

There's Bridget! Siobhan too. I smile and wave across the hall at Bridget and ignore sss. Mum sees their mother, and goes to talk to her. I have to be polite and stand there while sss smiles pityingly at my old jeans, parka and sneakers, looking down her stupid snub nose at me. I pull down my cricket cap and hide under the peak. She looks about twenty-five, in black tights and black shiny boots, a red mini skirt and black leather jacket, her hair done up in about a hundred tiny plaits and real holly-covered combs. I hope they prick her scalp and she gets tetanus.

Grandma used to say that if you can't find something nice to say about someone, say nothing. I don't think it applies to murderous thoughts though.

Bridget hugs me around the waist and we wander around together looking for presents. She tells me she has already got my present. Something she made. She's desperate to tell me what it is, but I stop her. I love surprises. She's wearing a hair band with reindeer antlers sticking up and a brooch with a flashing Santa. (He lights up, I mean.) I ask her if she's going to visit Santa Claus.

'No way, he's a fake. They're everywhere. There's one in the Lelant garden centre and at least two in Truro. The real Father Christmas lives in Lapland. I've sent him a letter.'

I stop at the bookstall and get lost in a book about bees. I don't know a thing about bees. It's time I did. However, I am not supposed to be looking for things for me, but for people on my list. I find a book about wildlife walks in Cornwall for Brett. I hope he hasn't got it already.

We have already made loads of jars of pickled onions, and Mum had some pickled samphire left over from the lot we made when we were at Peregrine Cottage. We are giving Mr and Mrs Lorn pickled onions, and samphire to Alistair and the Darlings. I buy some pickled walnuts as a treat for Mum. Mum has been very busy baking mince pies and a cake and a Christmas pudding, though I don't know why she makes a pudding because neither of us likes them. She never used to make cakes and stuff when we lived with Daddy. She's gone domestic since moving here.

I find three red fake fur mice with bells on for my cats. They like toys that rattle or squeak or make a noise when they 'kill' them.

Bridget is easy. When she is busy looking on a different stall I buy her a very pretty felt shoulder bag on a string. It's in the shape of a cat's face, and has whiskers. The stall sells cushions and tablecloths, holly wreaths and candles and embroidered glasses cases. I can't find anything pretty enough for Mum, though, but I am inspired to make something.

Mum wins a tin of talcum powder in the raffle. She'll give it to Mrs Thomas. Shame about the whisky. She buys some fairings – Cornish biscuits.

A successful Fair Mo, I think.

The air is warm for December and there's no sign of snow, I'm glad to say. I never enjoy the cold. I just go numb and my fingers and toes don't seem to belong to me.

When/if I ever get the transplant, I expect I'll put on weight and my circulation should be one hundred per cent better and I'll be able to go out in the snow. There'll be hundreds of pills to take every day, of course, to stop my body rejecting the new organs, but I'll eventually be able to run and climb and do sports again. It'll be brilliant. Maybe I'll learn how to play cricket.

Apparently one in three transplants don't go ahead on the first occasion, and one person we heard about had had seven cancellations before he had his operation.

Mum says Daddy is coming for Christmas! I can't believe it. Well, not for Christmas Day, but he's coming to visit between Christmas and New Year. I'm amazed Mum has agreed to it. I can't wait. Perhaps he'll stay for the New Year's Eve celebrations. There's going to be a huge firework display and everyone wears fancy dress and goes onto the streets and harbour for an all night party.

I'm making a specs-holder for Mum. I have invented the design. It's like one of those hanging shoe-storers, with pockets for each shoe, but mine is made of deckchair canvas, with separate stapled pockets for each pair of glasses. There's a hole at the top so she can hang it by the door or somewhere so she'll always know where to find them.

My main presents to people are photographs I've made. I've got a mounted black and white print of the three cats for Daddy, as I'm sure he must miss them terribly, living all on his own. I'm also writing him a copy of 'Cherish', hoping it will make him think of Mum. I'm sending Summer a photo of the view from my window, so she'll want to come here and visit. I've got a picture of the singing starling, which I've made into a card for Brett. For Mum I've made a rather good black and white still-life photograph of her grandfather's medal and I've coloured it in parts with watercolour paints, so it looks like art. I found cheap wooden frames the right size in a local shop and I've framed the prints.

Flo's helping – sorting out wrapping paper and ribbons for me and chasing them all over the floor so they don't escape. Charlie, who has no sense of humour or fun, sits on my bed and looks down her pink nose at Flo's undignified behaviour. Rambo is frightened of the noise Flo and I make with tissue paper and sellotape and hides under Mum's bed.

Our Christmas tree sits in a bucket covered with red and green wrapping paper. The room smells of pine. We've put the coloured fairy lights on it – the same lights we've always used, little plastic bells with nursery rhyme figures on them. No tasteful all-white or all-silver decorations for us. No way. If you can't be vulgar at Christmas, when can you? Oh, dear, I'm beginning to sound like my mother.

We have Grandpop and Grandma's old tree decorations this year. They have always been packed in cotton wool in a square biscuit tin with a picture on the lid of a little girl with yellow curls and a red dress playing with her dolls. The decorations are fragile, light as air, pure glass in lovely colours, pale pink, powder blue, scarlet, opal green. Some are balls, others like miniature bunches of grapes. I hang these baubles and try not to knock off too many pine needles. Silver strands are hung over the branches to add the finishing touch, and they glint and twinkle under the lights.

'Shall I put the fairy on top?'

From the tin Mum produces a hideous one-eyed, half-bald, one-armed half naked doll.

'If you must.'

'It was mine when I was little. She's called Tinkerbell.'

'Go on then,' I say, and she reaches up and slips the maimed fairy on the topmost branch.

'What about Santa?' I take out the little knitted Santa Claus that Grandma made and Mum positions it just beneath the fairy. I switch off the main light and we admire the pretty picture the tree makes in the bay window. Mum suddenly hugs me to her, and I can feel wetness on her cheek.

CHAPTER FORTY-TWO

I OVERHEAR THIS and I don't think I am supposed to: I'm sitting by my open window, camera in hand, waiting for inspiration. The weather is so mild we haven't even got the heating on. The starling is sitting in its usual place on the telegraph wire saying his prayers to the great Sky God, perhaps praying for a white Christmas. Mum is hanging out the washing, when Mrs Thomas from next door comes out.

Mum: 'Hello, my dear. Lovely weather, isn't it?' Why do adults always talk about the weather? It's pointless. Weather just is. Nothing we can do about it, so why even mention it? 'How are you, Marigold?'

Marigold! What a lovely name. She doesn't look like a Marigold, more like a Violet.

Mrs T: ''Es, I'm not too bad, you know, my 'ip and knees, as ever. Waiting for an appointment for my cataracts. 'Es. How 'bout you, my girl? How's your problem? Look peaky, you do.'

Mum: 'You were right, quite right – fibroids. Needs an operation.'

Mrs T: 'Tsk! Tsk! Tsk! Oo's goin' to look after the little maid then?'

Mum: 'Oh, I won't have it. It'll have to wait.'

It's evening and we are watching *Absolutely Fabulous*. We both love it.

'Mum, what did the doctor say when you saw him?'

'Her, my doctor's a woman.'

'Oh, right, what did she say?'

'Oh nothing, it's my age, hormones, fibroids, nothing much.'

'Do you need an operation?'

'No, I'll be all right, she's given me some tablets.'

Next day when Mrs T comes into the garden to hang up her smalls (isn't that a sweet expression for rather big knickers?) I am ready, armed with my camera. Mum's gone down town, last minute Christmas shopping.

'Hello my cheel', how're you then? Behavin' are you?'

'Mrs Thomas, may I take a photo of you please?'

'What for you want a picture of me?'

'For my portfolio.'

'That sounds important, portfolio. Go on then.'

I go into her garden and position her against the hedge of valerian. It's still flowering. She is of course wearing the flower-patterned apron, which acts as camouflage.

I have transparency film in the camera.

'Thank you Mrs Thomas, you look lovely.'

'You'm a funny maid, you are, taking a picture of an old lady like me.'

'Mrs Thomas, my mum isn't well, is she?'

'No, no, she isn't well.'

'It isn't cancer, is it? She isn't going to die?'

'Good heavens, no, my cheel'. She's got fibroids, that's all. Needs an operation, is all.'

'You sure?'

'Don't you go worrying about your mother, now, my girl, she's strong as an ox.'

'Thank you, Mrs Thomas.' I have to sniff loudly and blow my nose. 'Is there anything I can do for you?'

I was dreading she would want me to do some shopping but luckily she says no.

She sits on her front doorstep on a cushion in the sun, and her cat comes out and stands next to her, his back and tail arched in ecstasy as she strokes him. I've noticed before, she strokes him all the time, almost obsessively, as if her life depended on it. Shandy's like her lifebelt and she has to hold onto him or drown.

I imagine it must be very difficult to carry on living when everyone you love is dead.

This afternoon I go to the library to get a pile of books to read over Christmas and automatically ask to renew the lost books. The chatty lady looks at her files and says she can't renew them until I bring the books in for them to see.

Oho! The shit's hit the fan.

I obviously look shocked, because she says, 'I can renew them, but it's County Council policy to ask to see the books after they've been out a certain length of time.'

'Oh dear, the fact is, you see, Mum's... had an accident with them.'

She raises her eyebrows.

'Yes, an accident.' My mind is racing. What can I say? 'A dog, two dogs, a very aggressive bull terrier and a... a poodle, attacked her and tore the books to ribbons, I'm afraid, and ate them. She was only slightly injured but her mind was affected.'

I think she believes me.

'I see, the dogs have eaten the books. How novel. Well, perhaps you could ask Mummy to come and see us, because there will be a fine to pay.'

'A fine?'

'Yes.'

'How much will it be?'

'I'll have to check.'

She goes away and telephones someone.

'They weren't new books, dear, so ten pounds will cover it.'

Ten pounds! I give her the remains of my Christmas present money, all ten pounds of it. I can feel myself blushing with embarrassment, but relief too. Whew! I'll never ever tell a lie again.

'You don't have to pay it now, dear. The County Council will send her a letter.'

'No, no, that's fine, that's okay. She would want me to pay now. Really.'

She makes me wait while she writes a receipt.

Ten pounds. Thank goodness I have already got most of the presents. I'll make the rest.

Next day I wait for the post and it's Eugene, our old postie from Peregrine Cottage. He remembers me. I give him a hug and wish him Happy Christmas. Mum invites him in for a mince pie and a glass of wine and he eats and drinks standing up in the kitchen. He says they are short of postmen this Christmas and he's covering this part of town now. He has brought a load of Christmas cards for us. There's a card for me from Summer, with a photo of her and two other girls from my London school, taken in a photo booth. They look so happy and carefree and I miss them all suddenly, having not thought about them at all for months.

Hurray for darling Daddy, who sends me a Christmas card, a letter, and thirty pounds for Christmas expenses. Nineteen-year-old Luk from Thailand is history, it's someone called Natasha now. He doesn't give her age. Mum hoots and says he's incorrigible. She doesn't even sound bitter.

CHAPTER FORTY-THREE

I'M BACK AT Arts and Artists, and I ask to see the book about Arts and Crafts. It's a big book and the man gets it down for me. I sit at a desk and open the book.

Later, I phone Alistair.

CHAPTER FORTY-FOUR

ONLY FIVE MORE windows to open in the Advent calendar. I'm probably too old to have one really but go along with it for Mum's sake. She likes to make everything as Christmassy as possible.

The holiday people arrived last night. Daisy and Grace stroke our cats, who are all sunbathing in their garden. Grace is a bit younger than me but about four inches taller. I don't think she and her sister get on very well. I heard them squabbling through the wall. I've always wanted a sister but maybe it's not such a good idea. You can't choose who to have as family, you can only choose friends.

We've invited them all to come round on Christmas Day.

We are at a lunchtime party at Brett's house. We nearly didn't come because Mum is feeling lousy and doesn't feel up to socialising and Really Needs to be Near a Bathroom. It was only when she saw me all dressed up ready to go that she made an effort to get herself ready. She looks rather pale but very smart in a black dress and boots with a long string of red and green glass beads.

I have Brett's present with me to give him. We've got a box of cocoa-covered almonds and a bottle of Australian wine for Hayley and Steve from the two of us, and a big bag of seeds for their bird feeders.

I have new khaki baggy trousers and a long sleeved black T-shirt with sparkly red bits on it. Mum spent loads in Truro on clothes and I got these and a pair of red Doc Martens – an early Christmas present. My hair is newly trimmed and gelled into individual spikes. No hat. Mum says I look like a fetching urchin!

'What's fetching?'

'Pretty.'

That's going a bit far, but I do look a little more human than usual, I suppose.

They have a huge tree that hits the ceiling of their sitting room. I'm glad Steve hasn't insisted on a barbecue today, though it is still very mild. There are loads of guests I don't recognise, as they've made many friends at the school. Mum knows a few people, including Alistair, of course, who looks rather handsome in a black shirt and cords with an orange and pink tie. He drove us here.

The beach family is here, the godfather family. I say hello to the little fairy girl and ask her about Wobert. I think he's called Robert but she's not good on Rs.

'He's fine, spends his days on a sheepskin next to the fire keeping warm.'

Brett and I go into the garden to say hello to Buddy, who peers down at me suspiciously for a while then flops down to land on Brett's shoulder. He lets me stroke his shiny head – Buddy I mean. Brett talks soothingly to him, telling him how beautiful he is. He is so good with birds.

I imagine I am Buddy the raven, being lovingly caressed by Brett. I push my beak into his hand and croon like a pigeon. He strokes my flight feathers and I flutter them at him. Stop it, you idiot, I tell myself.

'Gussie,' Brett says, as Buddy flies back to his tree.

'Yes?'

'Nothing... I like... your DMs.'

'Brett?'

'Yeah?'

'Is Siobhan coming today?'

'Na, she's not coming.'

'Do you, are you, is she...?'

'She's a drongo, Guss, a dero, she's a waste of space.'

'Oh Brett, do you really think so?'

'Yeah, I like you much more.'

He gives me a high five and pats me on the head, and doesn't mind the gel.

We are at the St Ives Youth Theatre Christmas show with Claire, Gabriel and Troy. Gabriel sits next to me and can't wait to tell me his news. They've got the little black puppy. When I tell him that Mum and I found her and took her to the vet he looks adoringly at me as if I am his hero – heroine.

'What's her name, then?'

'Zennor.'

'And what do the cats think of her?'

'They've kept out of her way. She bounces too much.'

I nearly didn't recognise Phaedra as her hair is pulled up on top of her head and her make-up is extreme – green and purple streaks and black lips. She has to change costumes three times, and looks great in spangled tights, leotards and high heels. She's a wonderful singer and dancer.

In the interval I spot the man and woman I sat next to in the church, and in the second half I recognise their little girl in the show. It's such good fun, but it goes on a bit too long for me, and I don't like the dry ice smoke or whatever it is. But we all sing a few Christmas songs together at the end, like 'I'm Dreaming of a White Christmas' and 'Jingle Bells' and I feel suddenly festive and in the right Christmas spirit.

CHAPTER FORTY-FIVE

THIS VERY EMBARRASSING conversation has just taken place:

Mum – Gussie – I want to talk to you.

Me – Yeah?

Mum – I know about the funeral.

Me – Funeral? Oh.

Mum – Yes.

Me – So?

Mum – Well, do you want to talk about it?

Me – Not really.

Tears come suddenly and once I start I can't stop. Mum takes me in her arms and holds me tight. My scar hurts where she presses me to her but I don't complain.

And the whole story about the books comes out. I can't wait to tell her. I feel much better once I've admitted it. Guilt is too big a burden. She's remarkably understanding, and even laughs when I tell her about the tramp spotting me.

'Gussie, I do understand about you wanting to find a family, but sweetheart, you are not just a tiny fragment of a Stevens clan, you are you, unique, the one and only, and no one else is like you. You aren't a piece of family jigsaw; you are wonderfully yourself.'

'But Mum…'

'No, Gussie, listen to me, I know I'm only your Mum, and naturally I am biased, but you are my Marvellous Gussie, the sum of all your thoughts and dreams, your amazing experiences, good and bad, the places you have been to, your love of Daddy and Grandpop and Grandma, and even the books you read, and the films you love, and Especially your Imagination, they are part of Who You Are. It all goes to make the One and Only Gussie. You know that, don't you?'

I am sobbing more than I have ever sobbed, not because of unhappiness, but because this is the first indication I've ever had that Mum actually loves me. No, that's not true, of course it isn't, but it's the first time she's explained myself to me. And it sounds like she really understands. And so it's a happy crying. Happiness comes in strange shapes.

I realise that this is an important moment, precious, and is as beautiful as anything can be – like the sight of a shooting star, or listening to piece of really good music. My mum loves me, and I feel a great happiness. Even though I am dreading more illness and breathlessness and feeling lousy, and I'm terrified about the operation, or worse, not having the operation, what matters is now. My Mum and me; being kind and understanding to each other, that's what matters.

When I ask her how she knows about me going to the funeral, she says it was Mrs Stevens, the elderly lady who sat next to her at the hairdressers, who told her. And Alistair said something about the tea-lady at the cricket match asking about me.

You can't hide anything in this town. Pick your nose and eat the bogey and everyone knows about it the same day.

CHAPTER FORTY-SIX

THE LOCAL BUTCHER delivers the knuckles of ham, free range turkey, sausage meat and bacon that Mum ordered and she is doing mysterious things to them; soaking the hams, cleaning the bird, cooking the giblets with lemon, onion and bay leaf, and making the stuffing. I have helped make breadcrumbs, chop parsley and generally get in the way. Mum loves all this domesticity. She says it makes her feel good about herself.

There are mince pies and sausage rolls on baking trays ready for tomorrow. We have invited all our new friends for a lunchtime drinks and nibbles party.

The Parish Church of St Eia is full of holly and candles, and children, about thirty of us, are gathered around the Christmas crib, kneeling or standing. The vicar starts to tell the story of Christmas. One very little girl kneeling at the front suddenly cries out, 'Where's the baby Jesus?' and the vicar says He's not been born yet. At last the baby is placed in the manger and the vicar tells the grownups, who are in the main body of the church, that only the children are going to sing 'Away in a Manger'.

Mum's getting out her handkerchief in readiness. What is it about small children singing this carol that makes even grown men weep?

We all hold candles, even the little ones and I worry that they'll set fire to the straw that's scattered on the flagstones. Bridget's eyes are sparkling in the candlelight. Gabriel is here too, frowning at the model cows and sheep by the manger. We all sing the first verse. The vicar asks if anyone would like to sing a solo of the first verse. Bridget immediately puts her hand up. She stands and sings.

Away in a manger, no crib for a bed,
the little Lord Jesus laid down his sweet head.
The stars in the night sky look down where he lay
the little Lord Jesus asleep in the hay.

The vicar thanks her and asks if anyone would like to sing the second verse. A girl of about nine sings it haltingly. When the vicar asks if anyone would be brave enough to sing the third verse on their own, to my consternation Gabriel throws his hand up high. Who knows the words to the third verse, for goodness sake? My heart is in my throat, I feel so anxious on his behalf. No way would I offer to humiliate myself in front of all these people by singing a song I didn't know the words of. It's like that dream when you're in a play centre stage and you haven't learned your lines.

Little Gabriel stands up in front of me, candle flickering, and sings in a sweet piping voice:

The cattle are lowing, the babe He awakes
but little Lord Jesus no crying He makes.
I love you Lord Jesus! Look down from the sky
and stay by my side until morning is nigh.

Whew! He did it. I'm so proud of him.

We all sing the rest of the carol together, somehow remembering the words a millisecond after the adults. The last verse is:

Bless all the dear children
in Thy tender care,
and take us to heaven
to live with Thee there.

All the children and some of the adults carrying candles

put them on special candle sconces to one side of the chapel, chancel, whatever. I blow mine out because I like the smell. No one sets fire to the church.

We go home up Barnoon Hill, and have supper on our own – cheese on toast and a mince pie and clotted cream and hot chocolate. I have some last minute present wrapping to do, so does Mum.

I've made gift tags from old Christmas cards, using strands of silver foil as strings: a recycling technique I've inherited from Grandma. I am tired but I really really want to go out again to hear the carols sung in the streets of the old town late tonight.

We are wrapped in several layers of woolly clothes and hats and gloves and scarves. The waves are slithering darkly up the slipway. There are dead pigs in the doorways of the harbour front cottages. No they're not, they're sandbags. They do look just like pigs. The wind is getting up and the gulls are whirling and calling loudly. A ghost moon appears then disappears behind rushing clouds. A bright star. Then no stars.

Dozens of singers are gathering behind Piazza, a block of flats on Porthmeor beach. The dark courtyard is filled with excited voices, people jostling and greeting each other and laughing loudly. Everyone seems to know everyone else. Mum and I stand at the back under the shelter of a roofed carport.

There is a hush, only the sound of gulls screaming and the thump and whine of wind and sea. One man starts a low chanting call, the first line of a carol. The combined sound of about eighty singers rises and fills the courtyard, and our heads and minds and hearts. There are no musical instruments, just human sounds coming from throats, diaphragms and lips. Deep men's bass notes, rich tenors coming in behind and the piping sweetness of women's voices. It's beautiful. The harmonising sounds remind me of the funeral.

Three carols are sung and then the whole gathering moves off to another little square behind the old people's flats, beyond the Tate. Between carols the singers laugh and chatter. More singers arrive and bystanders like us. We can only listen, not knowing the strange carols with their local harmonies and repetitions. Some of the words are familiar but with unfamiliar tunes, like 'While Shepherds Watched'. I feel no cold tonight: I am filled with the warmth of the crush of people around me and the feeling of belonging and something like, I don't know... relijun.

The combined choirs of all the chapels in St Ives move together through the little cobbled streets and stop in the narrow lane that leads to Porthgwidden Beach. Bedroom windows open and people in pyjamas and dressing gowns open their doors to better hear the carols.

I hear one really old woman telling someone, 'I lived in this cottage since I was three. When we moved to the house there was no water – we 'ad to go with a pitcher to a public tap. There was no electric or gas. We 'ad an oil lamp in the kitchen and a small lamp or a candle to go to bed with. There was no flush toilets. Every night people emptied their bucket on the beach to dispose of that.'

It sounds like the dark ages to me. Then she says, 'There's hardly any local people left in the old cottages in Down'long. Holiday cottages now. Years ago they was condemned, unsanitary, and all the locals were moved uplong to council estate – "the reservation"– we called it.'

The wind is stronger now and her voice gets carried away into the night. We huddle on a step in a doorway. We listen to one more carol, 'In the Deep Mid-winter', Mum's favourite, and it starts to rain. Umbrellas go up and are blown inside out like ravens squabbling.

We leave reluctantly. The moon is hidden now and we walk through Fore Street where all the Christmas lights are swaying in the wind, the little trees lit up, and up Barnoon Hill, stopping to rest on the seat, huddling under the brolly. Mum hugs me close to keep me warm and holds my arm to help me up the rest of the way.

I am full of anticipation for tomorrow. Not just to see my presents, but to see Mum's face when she opens hers.

CHAPTER FORTY-SEVEN

I OPEN THE last little window of the Advent calendar and see the nativity scene, Mary and Joseph and the baby Jesus.

Word of the day for Christmas Day is *benign: favourable; gracious; kindly; of mild type.*

The wind and rain have gone, the sea is calm and a watery sun is shining. Mum is sitting on a cushion on the front doorstep having her first coffee and a fag. She turns and smiles at me.

'Happy Christmas, Mum.' I give her a big hug and kiss her face.

'Happy Christmas, sweetheart.'

The floor around our tree is covered in brightly coloured boxes and packages. Flo knocks a bauble from the lowest branch and smashes it on the skirting board. She looks very pleased with herself. Mum sweeps it into a dustpan and gets rid of it. I open the cats' presents and they have a lovely time chasing the paper and killing it. Rambo gets a piece of sellotape stuck to his fur and rushes off terrified, with it trailing behind him. Only Flo has the intelligence to play with her toy mouse, throwing it up and catching it between her paws and throwing it again.

'Can we open our presents yet?'

'Let's wait 'til after breakfast. Alistair is coming about 11, guests after 12.30.'

'What time is it now?'

'Half-nine.'

'Okay. That's not too long to wait. Can I open one present please? Just to keep me going?'

'Go on then.' She searches for her glasses and chooses a small package wrapped in gold tissue.

I open it and find a lovely little silver and white enamel brooch shaped like a seagull.

'Wow, thanks, Mum.'

'Car boot,' says Mum.

I make her open the box with the jar of pickled walnuts in and she is so pleased she eats one straight off.

The cats have caught the excitement in the air. After breakfast they follow her to the kitchen where she does disgusting things to our turkey. It reminds me of Grandma, who often had a hand up a plucked chicken's bottom.

I put some fresh peanuts and sunflower seeds into the bird feeder. Mrs Thomas has already been out hanging up washing and I wave to the girls next door. I can see them unwrapping presents in the front room. Luckily we have some extra presents for people we have forgotten – little sacks of chocolate coins wrapped in gold, and light-up Santa brooches from the Save the Children shop.

Flo, Rambo and Charlie have followed me out.

'Oh, I am so happy to be here!' says Flo, and grabs poor unsuspecting Charlie by the scruff of her neck.

'Shoo, bad cat. Where's your Christmas spirit? Good will to all cats and all that?'

Rambo is bravely sitting on the front step chattering to the starling carolling above on the telegraph wire.

Alistair arrives at the back door, his arms full of parcels and already cold champagne.

He hugs me and wishes me a happy Christmas. He smells nice, like lemons and heather and old tweed coats. He pours champagne, even for me, and we sit around the tree and I am Father Christmas handing out the presents. I give myself a small rectangular package. It's a little tape recorder with a microphone.

'That is so cool, thanks Alistair. Next Christmas, I can record the carols in the streets.'

Mum is pleased with the specs holder I made and hangs it in the kitchen next to the slate where we write shopping lists and things to remember.

Alistair gets a splendid green and blue striped tie and an antique blue enamel tie pin from Mum and a cricket diary from me.

She has a large bottle of her favourite smelly, Yves Saint Laurent's Y, from him and a long amber necklace that looks like a string of baked beans, or miniature yellow sausages, only shinier. She immediately takes off her red and green beads and wears the amber instead. It does look lovely against her black velvet dress.

I have a *Faber Book of Children's Verse*, a navy fleece hoodie, striped over-the-knee socks and a great khaki padded waistcoat with hundreds of pockets for film and lenses. And a gorgeous fake fur covered notebook and a pack of fibre tip pens.

Mum loves the hand-coloured photograph of her grand-father's *Croix de Guerre* and cannot believe I coloured it myself.

Dad has sent me film and a photograph album and a brilliant book on the portrait photographs of Jane Bowen.

Mum and Alistair look happy and are sitting on the sofa, his arm around her waist.

'Thanks, Mum, I love all my things,' I say and kiss her.

'You haven't opened the main present yet, sweetheart.'

'What? Where?' She points to several large boxes tucked behind the tree.

'Are those for me?' I scrabble with the paper and tape. I don't believe it! It's a computer! There's a printer and a keyboard, a screen and all sorts of other bits and pieces, wires and a mouse and mouse pad. There's even a ream of printing paper. It's a joint present from Mum and Daddy.

Alistair says he'll help set it all up for me tomorrow. I am overwhelmed. Now I can be a real writer.

'You haven't seen your main present yet, either,' I say to her and smile at Alistair, who winks at me, conspiratorially. 'It's from Alistair and me.'

I pass her the heavy parcel wrapped in gold and red paper with a big gold ribbon, saved from two years ago when it was wrapped around our Christmas cake.

Alistair pours more wine and we nibble walnuts and almonds.

'What is it? Shall I open it now or save it?'

'Open it now,' Alistair and I chorus.

She unwraps and folds the paper carefully, just like Grandma used to do, recycling for next year's presents. The second-hand book has a photograph of a handcrafted chair on the cover.

'Oh, this is nice, Gussie.'

I can see she is bemused (yesterday's word of the day, which I haven't had time to think about let alone use. It means: to put in confusion, to stupefy).

'Look on page 85,' I tell her.

There is a mention of my great-grandfather Amos Hartley Stevens, painter/photographer in St Ives and a short history of his life, mentioning the names of his children: Menzies, who died while he was still a baby; John, who died at sea when he was eighteen, and Fay, who became a painter and married James Darling, master craftsman and cabinet-maker; and Hartley, businessman.

'Now page 40,' I tell her.

James Darling, b1884 d1942. This master craftsman of Arts and Crafts domestic and architectural furniture married artist Fay Stevens (daughter of renowned Cornish photographer Amos Hartley Stevens, and Mary Menzies, novelist). One son – Amos.

'Fay? James Darling? Moss's Mum is your Grandfather

Hartley's sister?' Her eyes are wide. 'So we are related to the Darlings?'

'Yes, Mum, that's right. We are part of their family. And Dad's grandfather was the famous photographer, Amos Hartley Stevens, and Fay's son Moss (Amos) is named after him.

'How amazing! So Fay, Gabriel's gran, she's your great-aunt?'

'You would probably never have known if Gussie hadn't done the research,' said Alistair. 'I think this calls for another bottle of bubbly.'

CHAPTER FORTY-EIGHT

EVERYTHING IS SET; holly wreath on the front door, tree lights on, table set with starched white linen and lace, dishes and plates lined with lace doilies and full of nuts, fruit and goodies. The cats are all wearing red bows on their collars and looking, as Mum says, Like Butter Wouldn't Melt. I wish someone would explain that saying to me.

Arnold of the Holey Ears turns up with his very normal looking wife at the same time as Eugene, who is dressed as Santa Claus.

Mum, unbeknownst to me, has invited Ginnie. It's so lovely to see her. She gives me a hug and a subscription to the RSPB. I'll talk to her about Pop the herring gull later.

At the moment she's kissing Eugene under the mistletoe he brought with him.

Bridget and her family arrive – (excluding sss, who has a bad cold. Shame). Brett, Hayley and Steve arrive, laden with gifts for us, which they put under our tree for us to open later. Mrs Thomas, in her Sunday best, is staying to share our Christmas dinner. Mr and Mrs Lorn bring a bottle of whisky for Mum and a huge pack of chocolates for me. Our holiday neighbours are dressed in elaborate fancy dress – eighteenth century costume – in rehearsal for New Year's Eve, and last but not least all the Darlings arrive.

Phaedra and Troy stay long enough to hear our news that we are second cousins or whatever and then shoot off to ride the surf at Fistral Beach with friends who are waiting in Barnoon car park in their Beetle. Mum and Claire fall into each other's arms as if they are long lost sisters. Amos smiles benignly. Ha, I've used the word of the day.

Fay gives me a big kiss and says 'Welcome to our crazy

family, Gussie, and please call me Fay, not Auntie Fay or Great Aunt Fay, just Fay.'

She hugs me to her on one side, Gabriel on the other, and says, 'This is the best Christmas present I've ever had.'

Me too.

'Fay, could you tell me about my grandfather?'

'Hartley? Well, I hardly knew him, my dear, he was so much older than me. He'd left home when I was still a small child. We didn't see much of him really, he was always up to some get rich quick scheme. I think he was in Plymouth and Bristol, then he came home, married your grandmother, and ran a car sales company for a while.'

'And what about her?'

'Well, my parents didn't approve of her, I remember that. Bit of a gold digger, pretty, but no good for Hartley. He was weak you see, easily led.'

Later Daddy phones to say Happy Christmas. I thank him for the computer, and say Alistair is going to help set it up for me and tell him about the Darlings.

And guess what, Daddy's not coming after all. I don't even wait to hear his excuse. I don't care what it is. I don't care if he's broken a leg even. I don't care if he's broken both legs. I hand the phone to Mum without saying a word more to him.

'What is it?' she says, seeing my face.

'I knew it was all too good to last.' I go to my room.

CHAPTER FORTY-NINE

WE HAVE TO leave immediately.

My Life Call bleep goes off at 6 am. Mummy phones the transplant coordinator and they say there is a possible donor and we are to get there straight away.

Ohmygod, I don't believe it. A new heart and lungs! Mummy cries and hugs me. Alistair will drive us. He has a bigger faster car than us and has a week's leave.

Mrs Thomas will take all our left-over food, feed the cats today, and then the Lorns and Darlings will look after them until we get back home, which could be weeks or even months.

'Don't you worry about a thing,' she says, still in her dressing gown, in our kitchen, 'I'll see to the cats and everything.'

I think about Mrs Thomas's eighty-year-old heart. It's probably in a similar state of decay as mine, battered and bruised like an old balloon that's been kicked and punched too often and all the air has escaped and it's collapsing and wrinkled and can't float any more, but she's still very much alive and has plenty of fight in her.

And I think about the donor heart. Is it waiting in an icebox? Or is it still warm, beating inside a person who's been injured in a car crash, and the lungs kept pumping artificially by a machine? Are parents sitting holding the hands of their loved one, waiting for them to die? Did they have to give permission for the healthy organs to be used by someone else or did the dying person have an Organ Donor Card?

Mum tries to phone Daddy but he's not there.

I pack Rena Wooflie, my cricket cap, pyjamas, flip-flops, T-shirts and baggy trousers. It's always very warm in hospital.

It's like packing for a desert island. What books shall I take? I pack *The House at Pooh Corner*. Charlie tries to sit in the suitcase on top of the clothes: she wants to come with me. Oh, Charlie, I wish you could.

Mrs Thomas stands at the door waving and the cats are sulking at the window. Heavy rain falls, but the sun is shining from between two enormous black clouds, a shaft of light pooling the town. I look over my shoulder at the huddle of houses sparkling white, the little harbour where swirling gulls laugh and fret and a few boats swing on the choppy waves.

The Burying Beetle
Ann Kelley
ISBN 1 84282 099 0 PBK £9.99
ISBN 1 905222 08 4 PBK £6.99

The countryside is so much scarier than the city. It's all life or death here.

Meet Gussie. Twelve years old and settling into her new ramshackle home on a cliff top above St Ives, she has an irrepressible zest for life. She also has a life-threatening heart condition. But it's not in her nature to give up. Perhaps because she knows her time might be short, she values every passing moment, experiencing each day with humour and extraordinary courage.

Spirited and imaginative, Gussie has a passionate interest in everything around her and her vivid stream of thoughts and observations will draw you into a renewed sense of wonder.

Gussie's story of inspiration and hope is both heartwarming and heartrending. Once you've met her, you'll not forget her. And you'll never take life for granted again.

Gussie fairly fizzles with vitality, radiating fun and enjoyment into everything that comes her way. Her life may be predestined to be short but not short on wonder, glee, the love of things as they really are. It is rare to find such tragic circumstances written about without an ounce of self-pity. Rarer still to have the story of a circumscribed existence escaping its confines by sheer force of personality, zest for life.
MICHAEL BAYLEY

Luath Press Limited

committed to publishing well written books worth reading

LUATH PRESS takes its name from Robert Burns, whose little collie Luath (*Gael.*, swift or nimble) tripped up Jean Armour at a wedding and gave him the chance to speak to the woman who was to be his wife and the abiding love of his life. Burns called one of the 'Twa Dogs' Luath after Cuchullin's hunting dog in Ossian's *Fingal*.

Luath Press was established in 1981 in the heart of Burns country, and is now based a few steps up the road from Burns' first lodgings on Edinburgh's Royal Mile. Luath offers you distinctive writing with a hint of unexpected pleasures.

Most bookshops in the UK, the US, Canada, Australia, New Zealand and parts of Europe, either carry our books in stock or can order them for you. To order direct from us, please send a £sterling cheque, postal order, international money order or your credit card details (number, address of cardholder and expiry date) to us at the address below. Please add post and packing as follows: UK – £1.00 per delivery address; overseas surface mail – £2.50 per delivery address; overseas airmail – £3.50 for the first book to each delivery address, plus £1.00 for each additional book by airmail to the same address. If your order is a gift, we will happily enclose your card or message at no extra charge.

Luath Press Limited
543/2 Castlehill
The Royal Mile
Edinburgh EH1 2ND
Scotland
Telephone: 0131 225 4326 (24 hours)
Fax: 0131 225 4324
email: sales@luath. co.uk
Website: www. luath.co.uk